MY FAVOURITE SEA STORIES

Also in this series

MY FAVOURITE CAR STORIES
edited by Stirling Moss

MY FAVOURITE ANIMAL STORIES
edited by Gerald Durrell

MY FAVOURITE STORIES OF EXPLORATION
edited by David Attenborough

MY FAVOURITE STORIES OF WILD LIFE
edited by Peter Scott

MY FAVOURITE COUNTRY STORIES
edited by Henry Williamson

MY FAVOURITE STORIES OF TRAVEL
edited by Eric Newby

MY FAVOURITE HORSE STORIES
edited by Dorian Williams

MY FAVOURITE DOG STORIES
edited by Douglas Bader

My Favourite
SEA STORIES

edited by
ALAN VILLIERS

with drawings by
MARK MYERS

LUTTERWORTH PRESS
GUILDFORD AND LONDON

ISBN 0 7188 1709 5

*Printed in Great Britain at the St. Ann's Press
Park Road, Altrincham, Cheshire WA*14 5*QQ*

Acknowledgements

The editor is indebted to the following for permission to include material which is their copyright :

The Honourable Company of Master Mariners, for "Ordeal", by Angus MacDonald, from *Touching the Adventures,* ed. J. Lennox Kerr, published by George G. Harrap & Co. Ltd.

William Blackwood & Sons Ltd., for "Stern First", from *Down to the Sea* by Shalimar (F. C. Hendry)

Mr. Colin Martyr, for "The Life-Story of a Schooner", from *The South Seaman,* by Weston Martyr, published by William Blackwood & Sons Ltd.

Mr. Richard Lightoller, for "A Great Ship Dies", from *Titanic and other Ships,* by Comdr. Lightoller, published by Ivor Nicholson & Watson

J. M. Dent & Sons Ltd., and the Trustees of the Joseph Conrad Estate, for "The Character of the Foe", from *The Mirror of the Sea,* by Joseph Conrad

The Saturday Review, for "Gipsy Moth Circles the World" by Alan Villiers

Messrs. A. P. Watt & Son, and the Estate of the late Morley Roberts, for "The Promotion of the Admiral", from *The Promotion of the Admiral* by Morley Roberts, published by Eveleigh Nash

Mrs. James S. Learmont, for "Master in Sail", from *Master in Sail,* by Captain James S. Learmont, published by Percival Marshall

The Society of Authors as the literary representative of the Estate of John Masefield, for "Rounding the Horn", an extract from *Dauber* by John Masefield

John Murray (Publishers) Ltd., for "The Man who Made his own Passport", from *Escape to the Sea* by Fred Rebell

Gerald Duckworth & Co. Ltd., for "A Hot Cargo", from *The Brassbounder* by David. W. Bone.

Contents

Introduction   8

1. ORDEAL   11
   by Angus MacDonald from *Touching the Adventures*

2. STERN FIRST   35
   from *Down to the Sea* by Shalimar (F. C. Hendry)

3. LIFE-STORY OF A SCHOONER   63
   from *The South Seaman* by Weston Martyr

4. A GREAT SHIP DIES   77
   from *Titanic and Other Ships* by Comdr. Lightoller

5. THE CHARACTER OF THE FOE   88
   from *The Mirror of the Sea* by Joseph Conrad

6. GIPSY MOTH CIRCLES THE WORLD   91
   A Review by Alan Villiers

7. THE PROMOTION OF THE ADMIRAL (Abridged)   97
   from *The Promotion of the Admiral* by Morley Roberts

8. MASTER IN SAIL   121
   from *Master in Sail* by Captain James S. Learmont

9. ROUNDING THE HORN   127
   from *Dauber* by John Masefield

10. THE MAN WHO MADE HIS OWN PASSPORT   131
    from *Escape to the Sea* by Fred Rebell

11. A HOT CARGO   149
    from *The Brassbounder* by David W. Bone

INTRODUCTION

THE SEA has inspired poets and writers through the centuries. Who am I to make a selection among them when so many are so moving? I have stuck to the era I know—the last phase of the great sailing-ship, adventurous always and sometimes terrible. She developed to her greatest only in my life-time and now she is gone as utterly as if the wind had died for ever. She tested souls. She tried men and she moved them to write and to paint. She could suddenly offer them life-and-death testing: and slowly, reflective peace, too. When the least literary shipmaster took up his pen to record what he had just survived or was still happening round him, his plain prose could be eloquent indeed. Here is Captain James Middleton, master of the clipper *Fiery Cross* on a Yokohama voyage, caught in a typhoon in the China Sea.

"Blowing terrific with awful sea and torrents of rain," he writes with difficulty in the salt-stained Log under date Dec. 9, 1871. "Ship labouring, taking terrific seas over fore and aft. Midnight close-reefed main tops'l and mizzen staysail—last canvas set—blew away. Lashed cloth in weather rigging to keep her head to wind. Wind roaring like thunder and sea awful to look at . . . ship completely under water, all bulwarks gone, all livestock washed away . . . At noon same . . . Longboat gone . . . stove . . . expecting every minute masts to go . . . "

But they didn't go. Next Log entry is at New York, about three deserters. The little clipper recovered from the terrible typhoon.

8

Read Conrad for details of such a storm he encountered. I could take Conrad alone and produce a great collection—moving, memorable, compact with truth and feeling. I have chosen here rather the little-known and the unknown—the unorthodox adventurers. Men such as the strange Latvian who wrote his own passport, covered a Sydney harbour skiff with a bit of canvas and sailed off across the Pacific to California. Rebel indeed! No newspaper on earth cared two hoots about him: he had no contracts and wanted none. I applaud his spirit. Richard Hughes helped him a little to write his simple book.

The quiet Able Seaman Angus MacDonald ranks among the true heroes in this world, too, with his story "Ordeal". No writer either, he sat down one day in the Liverpool office of the Seafarers' Education Service and, scribbling away in a Woolworth exercise book, wrote the classic open-boat story of World Wars 1 and 2: and Dr. Ronald Hope, Director of that Service, recognised it. Angus MacDonald is real and has the touch to inspire, too . . . Such are my writers: and Weston Martyr, that cheerful chronicler of the sailing world before it went big-business (no fault of its own); the sea-dog who called himself "Shalimar" and knew his stuff from the deck up; Morley Roberts, who dealt with truth in dreadful times when sailors were literally stolen by fiendish men called "crimps" and sent drugged aboard outward-bound Cape Horners short of crew: old Captain Learmont of the *Brenda* and the *Bengairn*, who knew about that world and got magnificent performances out of splendid ships by other means. Lightoller was the senior surviving officer from the TITANIC: he swam. Captain David W. Bone was a windjammer 'prentice in the tough old days who became a liner master: and he could write, too. And John Masefield? Masefield *was* the Dauber in that poem—make no doubt of that. He wrote: he didn't paint. But he did the feeling: the accidents were not imagery, but recorded by a great imagination stirred to expression in a storm-tossed, fighting four-masted barque . . .

These are my writers—these and that most courageous man Francis Chichester. He fits in with them.

Alan Villiers

I *Ordeal*

ANGUS MacDONALD

THE ship I served on board, the Ellerman Liner *City of Cairo*, left Bombay on the 2nd of October, 1942, homeward bound with a crew of Europeans and lascars and a hundred passengers. At 8.30 p.m. on the 6th day of November, five days after leaving Cape Town, she was torpedoed by a German submarine. Three passengers and eighteen members of the crew were killed by the explosion of the torpedoes or went down with the ship.

I was a quartermaster and had charge of No. 4 lifeboat. After seeing everything in order there and the boat lowered, I went over to the starboard side of the ship to where my mate, quartermaster Bob Ironside, was having difficulty in lowering his boat. I climbed inside the boat to clear a rope fouling the lowering gear, and was standing in the boat pushing it clear of the ship's side as it was being lowered, when a second torpedo exploded right underneath and blew the boat to bits. I remember a great flash, and then felt myself flying through space, then going down and down. When I came to I was floating in the water, and could see all sorts of wreckage around me in the dark. I could not get the light on my life-jacket to work, so I swam towards the largest bit of wreckage I could see in the darkness. This turned out to be No. 1 lifeboat and it was nearly submerged, having been damaged by the second explosion. There were a few people clinging to the gunwale, which was down to water-level, and other people were sitting inside the flooded boat.

I climbed on board, and had a good look round to see if the boat was badly damaged. Some of the gear had floated away, and what was left was in a tangled mess. There were a few lascars, several women and children, and two European male passengers in the boat, and I explained to them that if some of them would go overboard and hang on to the gunwale or the wreckage near us for a few minutes we could bail out the boat and make it seaworthy. The women who were there acted immediately. They climbed outboard and, supported by the life-jackets everyone was wearing, held on to an empty tank that was floating near by. I felt very proud of these women and children. One woman (whose name, if I remember rightly, was Lady Tibbs) had three children, and the four of them were the first to swim to the tank. One young woman was left in the boat with two babies in her arms.

We men then started to bail out the water. It was a long and arduous task, as just when we had the gunwale a few inches clear, the light swell running would roll in and swamp the boat again. Eventually we managed to bail out the boat, and then we started to pick up survivors who were floating on rafts or just swimming. As we worked we could see the *City of Cairo* still afloat, but well down in the water, until we heard someone say, "There she goes." We watched her go down, stern first, her bow away up in the air, and then she went down and disappeared. There was no show of emotion, and we were all quiet. I expect the others, like myself, were wondering what would happen to us.

We picked up more survivors as the night wore on, and by the first light of dawn the boat was full. There were still people on the rafts we could see with the daylight, and in the distance were other lifeboats. We rowed about, picking up more people, among them Mr. Sydney Britt, the chief officer, and quartermaster Bob Ironside, who was in No. 3 boat with me when the second torpedo struck. Bob's back had been injured, and one of his hands had been cut rather badly. We picked up others, then rowed to the other boats to see what decision had been made about our future. Mr. Britt had, naturally, taken over command of our boat, and now he had a conference with Captain Rogerson, who was in another boat. They decided we would make for the nearest land, the island of St. Helena, lying five hundred miles due north. We transferred people from boat to boat so that families could be together. Mr. Britt suggested that, as our boat was in a bad way, with many leaks and a damaged rudder, and at least half its water-supply lost, all the children should shift to a dry boat and a few adults take their places in our boat.

When everything was settled we set sail and started on our long voyage. Our boat was now overcrowded with fifty-four persons on board—twenty-three Europeans, including three women, and thirty-one lascars. There was not enough room for everyone to sit down, so we had to take turns having a rest. The two worst injured had to lie down flat, so we made a place in the bows for Miss Taggart, a ship's stewardess, and cleared

a space aft for my mate, quartermaster Bob Ironside.
We did not know exactly what was wrong with Bob's
back. We had a doctor in the boat, Dr. Tasker, but he
was in a dazed condition and not able to attend to the
injured, so we bandaged them up as best we could with
the first-aid materials on hand. The youngest person
among us, Miss Diana Jarman, one of the ship's passengers, and only about twenty years of age, was a great
help with the first aid. She could never do enough, either
in attending to the sick and injured, boat work, or even
actually handling the craft. She showed up some of the
men in the boat, who seemed to lose heart from the
beginning.

Once we were properly under way Mr. Britt spoke to
us all. He explained all the difficulties that lay ahead,
and asked everyone to pull their weight in everything to
do with managing the boat, such as rowing during calm
periods and keeping a look-out at night. He also explained that as we had lost nearly half our drinking
water we must start right away on short rations. We
could get two tablespoonfuls a day per person, one in
the morning and one in the evening. He told us there
were no passengers in a lifeboat, and everyone would
have to take turns bailing as the boat was leaking very
badly.

Before noon on that first day we saw our first sharks.
They were enormous, and as they glided backward and
forward under the boat it seemed they would hit and
capsize us. They just skimmed the boat each time they
passed, and they were never to leave us all the time we
were in the boat.

The first night was quiet and the weather was fine,
but we didn't get much rest. A good proportion of us
had to remain standing for long periods, and now and
then someone would fall over in their sleep. I was in
the fore-part of the boat attending to the sails and the

running gear, helped by Robert Watts from Reading, whom we called "Tiny" because he was a big man. He didn't know much about seamanship, as he was an aeronautical engineer, but he said to me that first day, "If you want anything done at any time just explain the job to me and I'll do it." His help was very welcome as we did not have many of the crew available for the jobs that needed to be done. From the very beginning the lascars refused to help in any way, and just lay in the bottom of the boat, sometimes in over a foot of water.

On the second day the wind increased, and we made good speed. Sometimes the boats were close together and at other times almost out of sight of each other. Our boat seemed to sail faster than the others, so Mr. Britt had the idea that we might go ahead on our own. If we could sail faster than the others, and as we were leaking so badly, we should go ahead and when we got to St. Helena we could send help to the others. Mr. Britt had a talk with Captain Rogerson when our boats were close, and the captain said that if the mate thought that was the best plan then to go ahead. So we carried on on our own.

During the hours of darkness the wind rose stronger, and, as we could see the running gear was not in the best conditions, we hove to. As it got still worse, we had to put out a sea-anchor and take turns at the steering-oar to hold the boat into the seas. We had a bad night, and two or three times seas broke over the heavily laden boat and soaked us all to the skin. It was during this night that we noticed Dr. Tasker was failing mentally. Every now and then he shouted, "Boy, bring me my coffee," or, "Boy, another beer." He had a rip in his trousers, and in the crowded boat during the night he cut a large piece out of the trousers of the ship's storekeeper, Frank Stobbart. I noticed the doctor with the knife and a piece of cloth in his hand. He was trying to fit the cloth over his own trousers. I pacified him and took his knife, a small silver knife with a whisky advertisement on the side. I had the same knife all through the years I was a prisoner in Germany, and only lost it after the war while serving in another Ellerman liner.

At noon on the third day the wind abated, and we set sails again and went on. We had lost sight of the other boats now and were on our own. We all expected to see a rescue ship or plane at any time, but nothing turned up. On the evening of the fourth day the doctor got worse, and rambled in his speech. He kept asking for water, and once Mr. Britt gave him an extra ration, although there was not much to spare. During the night the doctor slumped over beside me, and I knew he was dead. That was the first death in the boat. We cast the body overboard at dawn while Mr. Britt read a short prayer. We all felt gloomy after this first burial, and wondered who would be next.

Later in the day I crawled over to have a yarn with my mate Bob, and he said, "Do you think we have a chance, Angus?" I said, "Everything will be all right, Bob. We are bound to be picked up." Bob hadn't long been married, and he was anxious about his wife and little baby in Aberdeen. He couldn't sit up, and I was afraid his back was broken or badly damaged.

Day and night the lascars kept praying to Allah, and repeating, "Pani, sahib, pani, sahib," and they would never understand that the water was precious and had to be rationed out. On the sixth morning we found three of them dead in the bottom of the boat. The old engine-room serang read a prayer for them, and Tiny and I pushed them overboard, as the lascars never would help to bury their dead. The only two natives who helped us at any time were the old serang, a proper gentleman, and a fireman from Zanzibar, and they couldn't do enough to help.

We were getting flat calms for long periods, and we lowered the sails and used the oars. We didn't make much headway, but the work helped to keep our minds and bodies occupied. I know that doing these necessary tasks helped to keep me physically fit and able to stand up to the ordeal that lay ahead. There were a few Europeans who never gave a helping hand, and I noticed that they were the first to fail mentally. They died in the first two weeks.

I was worried about Miss Taggart's sores, as they had now festered and we had nothing to dress them with except salt water. With her lying in the same position all the time her back was a mass of sores. Tiny knew more about first aid than the rest of us, and with the aid of old life-jackets he padded her up a bit. But on the seventh night she died and slipped down from her position in the bows. As she fell she got tangled up with another passenger, a Mr. Ball from Calcutta, and when we got things straightened out they were both dead. A few more lascars died during the same night, and we had to bury them all at daybreak. The sharks were there in shoals that morning and the water was churned up as they glided backward and forward near the bodies. Things were now getting worse on board, and a good few of the people sat all day with their heads on their chests doing and saying nothing. I talked to one young engineer, and told him to pull himself together as he was young and healthy and to take a lesson from Diana, who was always cheerful and bright. She had told us, "Please don't call me Miss Jarman; just call me Diana." The young engineer did pull himself back to normal but within two days he dropped back and gave up hope and died. As we buried the bodies the boat gradually became lighter and the worst leaks rose above the water-line, so there was not so much water to bail out, although we had still to bail day and night.

Our own ship's stewardess, Annie Crouch, died on the tenth day. She had been failing mentally and physically for a time, and persisted in sitting in the bottom of the boat. We shifted her to drier places, but she always slid back. Her feet and legs had swollen enormously. Her death left only one woman among us, Diana. She was still active and full of life, and she spent most of her time at the tiller. Mr. Britt was beginning to show signs of mental strain, and often mumbled to himself. If I asked him a question he would answer in a dazed sort of way. I worried about him a lot, for he was always a gentleman, and everyone thought the world of him. On the twelfth day he was unable to sit up or talk, so we laid him down alongside Bob Ironside, who was also failing fast. Bob called me over one day, and asked me if I thought there was still a chance. I said certainly there was, and urged him not to give up hope as he would soon be home. He said, "I can't hang on much longer, Angus. When I die, will you take off my ring and send it home if you ever get back?" There were only a few able-bodied men left among the Europeans now, and Tiny Watts, my right-hand man, died on the fourteenth morning. He hadn't complained at any time, and I was surprised when I found him dead. We buried seven bodies that morning: five lascars, Tiny, and Frank Stobbart. It took a long time to get them overboard, and I had to lie down and rest during the operation.

On the fifteenth morning at dawn both Mr. Britt and Bob were dead, also three other Europeans, and a few lascars. A few more lascars died during the day. One of the firemen said that if he couldn't get extra water he would jump overboard, and later in the day he jumped over the stern. He had forgotten to take off his life-jacket, and as we were now too weak to turn the boat round to save him, the sharks got him before he could drown. The remaining survivors voted that I should take over command. On looking through Mr. Britt's papers I could see the estimated distances for each day up to about the tenth day, but after that there were only scrawls and scribbles. When I checked up on the water I found we had enough only for a few days, so I suggested cutting down the issue to one tablespoonful a day. There were plenty of biscuits and malted-milk tablets, but without water to moisten the mouth the biscuits only went into a powder and fell out of the corner of the mouth again. Those people with false teeth had still more trouble as the malted-milk tablets went into a doughy mess and stuck to their teeth.

The boat was now much drier, and there was not so much bailing to do as we rode higher in the water and most of the leaks were above the surface. The movement, however, was not so steady as when we were heavier laden, but about the middle of the seventeenth night the boat appeared to become very steady again. I heard Diana cry out, "We're full of water," and I jumped up and found the boat half full of water. I could see the plug-hole glittering like a blue light, and I started looking for the plug. I put a spare one in place, and a few of us bailed out the water. There were two people lying near the plug-hole, and they seemed to take no interest in what was happening. About an hour later I discovered the plug gone again and water entering the boat. I put the plug back, and this time I lay down with an eye on watch. Sure enough, in less than half an hour I saw a hand over the plug pulling it out. I grasped the hand and found it belonged to a young European. He was not in his right mind, although he knew what he was doing. When I asked him why he tried to sink the boat he said, "I'm going to die, so we might as well go together." I shifted him to the fore part of the boat, and we others took turns in keeping an eye on him, but he managed to destroy all the contents of the first-aid box and throw them over the side. He died the next day, with seven or eight lascars, and a banker from Edinburgh, a Mr. Crichton. Mr. Crichton had a patent waistcoat fitted with small pockets, and the valuables we found there we put with rings and other things in Diana's handbag. Among Mr. Crichton's possessions were the three wise monkeys in jade and a silver brandy flask that was empty.

At the end of the third week there were only eight of us left alive in the boat: the old engine-room serang, the fireman from Zanzibar, myself, Diana, Jack Edmead, the steward, Joe Green from Wigan, Jack Oakie from Birmingham, and a friend of his Jack Little. Two of them had been engineers working on the new Howrah bridge at Calcutta.

There was still no rain. We had not had a single shower since we started our boat voyage, and the water was nearly finished. Only a few drops were left on the bottom of the tank. About the middle of the fourth week I was lying down dozing in the middle of the night when the boat started to rattle and shake. I jumped up, thinking we had grounded on an island. Then I discovered a large fish had jumped into the boat and was thrashing about wildly. I grabbed an axe that was lying handy, and hit the fish a few hard cracks. The axe bounded off it like rubber, and it was a while before I made any impression, but when it did quieten down I tied a piece of rope round the tail and hung the fish on the mast. It took me all my time to lift the fish, as it was about three feet long and quite heavy. I lay down again, and at daybreak examined the fish closer. It was a dog-fish. During the struggle with it I had gashed a finger against its teeth, and as we now had no bandages or medicine all I could do was wash the cut in sea water before I proceeded to cut up the fish. I had heard and read about people drinking blood, and I thought that I could get some blood from the carcass for drinking. I had a tough job cutting up the fish with my knife, and only managed to get a few teaspoonfuls of dirty, reddish-black blood. I cut the liver and heart out, and sliced some of the flesh off. By this time all hands were awake, although everyone was feeling weak. I gave the first spoonful of blood to Diana to taste, but she spat it out and said it was horrible. I tried everyone with a taste, but nobody could swallow the vile stuff. I tried it myself, but couldn't get it down. It seemed to swell the tongue. We tried eating the fish, but that was also a failure. I chewed and chewed at my piece, but couldn't swallow any and eventually spat it out into the sea.

The day following my encounter with the big dog-fish my hand and arm swelled up, and Diana said I had blood-poisoning. The following day it was much worse, and throbbed painfully. I asked Diana if she could do anything for it, as we had no medical supplies left. She advised me to let the hand drag in the water, and later in the day she squeezed the sore, and all sorts of matter came out. I then put my hand back in the water, and that seemed to draw out more poison. At intervals Diana squeezed the arm from the shoulder downward, and gradually got rid of the swelling, although the sore didn't heal for months, and the scar remains to this day.

There was no water left now, and Jack Oakie, Jack Little, and the Zanzibar fireman all died during the one night. It took the remainder of us nearly a whole day to lift them from the bottom of the boat and roll them overboard. The serang was now unconscious and Joe Green was rambling in his speech. There were a few low clouds drifting over us, but no sign of rain, and I had lost count of the days. I had written up Mr. Britt's log-book to the end of the fourth week, but after that day and night seemed to be all the same. Diana had the sickness that nearly everyone in turn had suffered: a sore throat and a thick yellow phlegm oozing from the mouth. I think it was due to us lying in the dampness all the time and never getting properly dry. The sails were now down and spread across the boat as I was too feeble to do anything in the way of running the boat. Against all advice, I often threw small quantities of sea water down my throat, and it didn't seem to make me any worse, although I never overdid it.

One night Joe Green would not lie in the bottom of the boat in comfort, but lay on the after end in an uncomfortable position. When I tried to get him to lie down with us he said, "I won't last out the night, and if I lie down there you will never be able to lift me up and get me over the side." The next morning he was dead. So was the serang. Two grand old men, though of different races. There were only three of us left now Jack Edmead was pretty bad by now, and Diana still had the sore throat. But we managed to get the bodies over the side. The serang by this time was very thin and wasted, and if he had been any heavier we would not have managed to get him over.

By this time we were only drifting about on the ocean. I had put the jib up a couple of times, but discovered we drifted in circles, so I took it down again. One day I had a very clear dream as I lay there in the bottom of the boat. I dreamed that the three of us were walking up the pierhead at Liverpool, and the dream was so clear that I really believed it would happen. I told Diana and Jack about the dream, and said I was sure we would be picked up. There wasn't a drop of water in the boat now, and the three of us just lay there dreaming of water in all sorts of ways. Sometimes it was about a stream that ran past our house when I was a child, another time I would be holding a hose and spraying water all round, but it was always about water. Jack was getting worse, and was laid out in the stern, while Diana was forward where it was drier. Sick as she was, she always used to smile and say, "We still have a chance if we could only get some rain."

Then one night rain came. I was lying down half asleep when I felt the rain falling on my face. I jumped up shouting, "Rain, rain," but Jack wasn't able to get up and help me. Diana was in pretty bad condition, but she managed to crawl along and help me spread the main sail to catch the water. It was a short sharp shower and didn't last long, but we collected a few pints in the sail and odd corners of the boat. We didn't waste a drop, and after pouring it carefully into the tank we sucked the rain-drops from the woodwork and everywhere possible. Diana had trouble swallowing anything as her throat was swollen and raw, but I mixed some pemmican with water, and we had a few spoonfuls each. The water was very bitter as the sail had been soaked in salt water for weeks, but it tasted good to us. We all felt better after our drink, and I sat down in the well of the boat that day and poured can after can of sea water over myself, and gave Diana a bit of a wash. She was in good spirits now, although she could only speak in whispers. She told me about her home in the South of England: I think she said it was Windsor, on the Thames. She was very fond of horses and tennis and other sports, and she said, "You must come and visit us when we get home," which showed that like myself she had a firm conviction that we would get picked up.

The three days after the rain were uneventful. Diana was a bit better, but Jack was in a bad way, and lying down in the stern end. On the third day I had another shower-bath sitting down in the boat, as it had livened me up a lot the last time. Afterward I set the jib and tried to handle the main sail, but couldn't make it, so I spread the sail and used it as a bed. I had the best sleep in weeks. In the early hours of the morning Diana shook

me, and said excitedly, "Can you hear a plane?" I
listened, and heard what sounded like a plane in the
distance, so I dashed aft and grabbed one of the red
flares and tried to light it. It didn't go off, so I struck
one of the lifeboat matches. It ignited at once, and I
held it up as high as I could, and immediately a voice
shouted, "All right, put that light out." It was still dark,
but on looking in the direction of the voice we could see
the dim outline of a ship, and hear the sound of her
diesel engines. The same voice shouted, "Can you come
alongside?" God knows how we managed, but manage
it we did. Even Jack found enough strength to give a
hand, and with Diana at the tiller he and I rowed the
boat alongside the ship. A line was thrown to us, and I
made it fast. A pilot ladder was dropped, and two men
came down to help us on board. They tied a rope round
Diana, and with the help of others on the ship hauled
her on board. I climbed up unaided, and the men helped
Jack. The first thing I asked for was a drink, and we sat
on a hatch waiting to see what would happen. We
thought we were on a Swedish ship at first, but I saw a
Dutch flag painted across the hatch. Then I heard a
couple of men talking, and I knew then we were on a
German ship, as I had a slight knowledge of the language. I told the other two, and Diana said, "It doesn't
matter what nationality it is as long as it is a ship."

A man came to us soon and asked us to go with him
and meet the captain. Two of the crew helped Diana
and Jack, and we were taken amidships to the doctor's
room, where a couch had been prepared for Diana. The
captain arrived, and asked us about our trip in the boat
and inquired how long we had been in it. I told him
our ship had been torpedoed on the 6th of November,
and that I lost count of the days. He said this was the
12th of December, and that we were on board the German ship *Rhakotis*, and we should be well looked after.

I remembered the bag of valuables in the boat, and told the captain where Diana's bag was. The bag was found and passed up, and given into the captain's charge. It was probably lost when the ship was sunk three weeks later. The lifeboat was stripped and sunk before the ship got under way again.

We were given cups of coffee, but were told that the doctor's orders were for us not to drink much at a time, and only eat or drink what he ordered. Diana was lying on the doctor's couch, and when the three of us were left alone for a while she bounced up and down on the springs and said, "This is better than lying in that wet boat." Later Jack and I were given a hot bath by a medical attendant, and my hand was bandaged, as it was still festering. We were taken aft to a cabin, and Diana was left in the doctor's room. The crew had orders not to bother us and to leave us on our own, as we had to rest as much as possible. When I looked at myself in the mirror I didn't recognize myself with a red beard and haggard appearance. There didn't seem to be any flesh left on my body, only a bag of bones. Jack looked even worse with his black beard and hollow cheeks.

We had been given some tablets and injected, and were now told to go to bed. Before I did so I asked one of the crew to fetch me a bottle of water. Although this was against the doctor's orders the man did so, and I hid the bottle under my pillow. Then I asked another man to bring me a bottle of water, and in this way I collected a few bottles and I drank the lot. Jack was already asleep when I turned in after drinking the water, and I turned in on the bunk above him. We slept for hours and when I awoke I found I had soaked the bedding. Later I discovered I had soaked Jack's bed too. He was still asleep. I wakened him and apologized, but he only laughed. The steward brought us coffee at 7 a.m., and when I told him about my bladder weakness he didn't seem annoyed, but took the bedclothes away to be changed. It was a year before I was able to hold any liquid for more than an hour or so.

We were well looked after and well fed on the German ship, and from the first day I walked round the decks as I liked. Jack was confined to bed for a few days. We were not allowed to visit Diana, but the captain came aft and gave us any news concerning her. She couldn't swallow any food, and was being fed by injections. When we had been five days on the ship the doctor and the captain came along to our cabin, and I could see they were worried. The captain did the talking, and said that as the English girl still hadn't been able to eat, and couldn't go on living on injections, the doctor wanted to operate on her throat and clear the inflammation. But first of all he wanted our permission. I had never liked the doctor and had discovered he was disliked by nearly everyone on board, but still, he was the doctor, and should know more about what was good for Diana than I could. So I told the captain that if the doctor thought it was necessary to operate he had my permission as I wanted to see Diana well again. Jack said almost the same, and the captain asked if we would like to see her. We jumped at the chance, and went with the doctor. She seemed quite happy, and looked well, except for being thin. Her hair had been washed and set, and she said she was being well looked after. We never mentioned the operation to her, but noticed she could still talk only in whispers.

That evening at seven o'clock the captain came to us, and I could see that something was wrong. He said, "I have bad news for you. The English girl has died. Will you follow me, please?" We went along, neither of us able to say a word. We were taken to the doctor's room where she lay with a bandage round her throat. You would never know she was dead, she looked so peaceful.

The doctor spoke, and said in broken English that the operation was a success, but the girl's heart was not strong enough to stand the anaesthetic. I couldn't speak, and turned away broken-hearted. Jack and I went aft again, and I turned into my bunk and lay crying like a baby nearly all night. It was the first time I had broken down and cried, and I think Jack was the same. The funeral was the next day, and when the time came we all went along to the foredeck where the ship's crew were all lined up wearing uniforms and the body was in a coffin covered by the Union Jack. The captain made a speech in German, and then spoke in English for our benefit. There were tears in the eyes of many of the Germans, as they had all taken an interest in the English girl. The ship was stopped, and after the captain had said a prayer, the coffin slid slowly down the slipway into the sea. It had been weighted, and sank slowly. The crew stood to attention bareheaded until the coffin disappeared. It was an impressive scene, and a gallant end to a brave and noble girl. We had been through so much together, and I knew I would never forget her.

The *Rhakotis* was bound for Bordeaux, and was due there about New Year's Day. We had a good Christmas at sea, with all sorts of food, and as I had regained my normal appetite by then I was able to take my share of everything. The butcher had killed two pigs, and we had as much roast pork as we could eat. I am sure we got a better Christmas as prisoners on the *Rhakotis* than many seamen had on British ships.

There was great excitement on board on the 31st of December, and word got round that we had a rendezvous with four U-boats who would escort us into port. We stopped at 7 p.m. that evening, and within a few minutes the subs came close alongside out of the darkness. Nobody stopped us looking over the side at them, and we saw a couple of officers come aboard and meet the captain. They didn't stay long, and within half an hour we were on our way again. The subs disappeared, but they must have been somewhere in the vicinity. At 4 a.m. on New Year's Day Jack woke me up and said, "Look at the yellow light on our deck." The whole ship was lit up, and when I went outside I saw a flare floating above the ship. Then I heard the drone of a plane, and the anti-aircraft guns opened up. The plane dropped a load of incendiaries and some bombs. A few incendiaries landed on the ship amidships, but I don't think they did much damage. After a time all went quiet again, and we turned in. Jack remarked that this was a good beginning to the New Year.

We were having a special dinner that afternoon at 4.30 p.m., when I heard an explosion I guessed was gunfire. Immediately loud alarm bells sounded, and armed guards appeared at the door. I asked one of them what was the matter, and he said simply, "English cruiser." We could hear the gunfire plainer now, and then we felt the ship being hit. The noise was terrific, and there were loud crashes not far from where we waited. An armed guard ran down the alleyway calling out, "To the boats." Others were unwinding a coil of electric flex and setting a box against the ship's side. This was a time-bomb to scuttle the ship after we got clear, but it was not required as the ship was on fire all over and badly damaged by direct hits. I didn't know from which side the shells were coming, so I picked the port-side boat, and no sooner got there than I saw the British cruiser a good way off on the port side. She was firing salvoes, and I could see the flashes and hear the shells screaming past. The weather was bad at the time, and a large swell was running, so it wasn't easy getting the boats away. I slid down a lifeline into the boat, and was no sooner in it than a large sea came along and partly submerged the boat. I had nothing to do with the handling of the boat as the Germans were all at their proper stations, but I helped to push it clear with a boathook. We were just clear when there was a shout from the *Rhakotis*, and we could see two men waving and shouting for us to come back. The ship had a big list, and was a mass of flames from stem to stern, but the boat was turned back, and the two men jumped into the water, and were dragged into the boat. Shells were exploding all around, and I expected any minute the boat would be hit. The cruiser kept firing until the *Rhakotis* was on her beam ends, then turned and went full speed away. She must have known there were U-boats in the vicinity. I was very disappointed, as I was so sure they would have picked us up. As their ship rolled over and went slowly down the Germans took off their caps and gave her three cheers.

We were now alone in the Bay of Biscay, and in darkness. The starboard boat was not in sight, and it was many years before I learned that Jack Edmead was in her, and that she managed to reach Spain. From there poor Jack was sent home, only to join a ship that was later torpedoed. There were thirty-five of us in the port boat, including a few prisoners. I was the only Britisher. Sitting beside me were two young Danish boys, only fifteen years of age, whose ship had been captured in the Indian Ocean. These boys had been good to Jack and me on the German ship, and they turned up at the prisoner-of-war camp where I was placed. After their release they sent me a few welcome parcels of food.

The boat was in good condition and well stocked with water and large biscuits. Although there was a tremendous sea running, she was fairly steady, and only once or twice did she take any water on board during that wild night. I had no hat on, and as it was New Year's Day and cold I looked round for something to put on my head. I could see a beret sticking out of one of the German's pockets, so I quietly drew it out and put it on. He was wearing a sou'wester and did not miss the beret.

The following morning the wind had died down a bit, but there was still a big sea running. The officer in charge took a chance and set sail for the nearest land on the French coast. We each had a handful of biscuits and a glass of water for breakfast, and we were quite happy. About eleven o'clock someone shouted out, "U-boat," and I could see the periscope coming up out of the water close to us. The conning-tower appeared, and then the sub itself showed up. The hatch opened, and the commander shouted to the officer in charge of our boat, giving instructions on how we were to transfer to the submarine. We took the boat as close as we dared without touching the sub, as bumping would have capsized us, and as the nose of the sub rose to the sea one man at a time grabbed a wire and was pulled on board. It took a long time to get us all transferred, and once on the sub we all threw our life-jackets away and went below. It was only a small submarine, returning to port after fourteen days hunting the Atlantic convoys when it was ordered by radio to find the two boats from the *Rhakotis*. As soon as we got below each man was given a large mug of steaming coffee laced with rum, then shown to a spot where he had to lie. The submarine was cramped enough with its own crew, and now with thirty-five extra men it was like a sardine-tin.

We were only submerged fifteen minutes when a harsh alarm bell rang, and the nose of the sub dipped as she crash-dived. A few seconds later there were three tremendous explosions. The first shook us, the second was worse, and the third must have been very close, for the whole sub shook, and we were thrown about. I fell off the bunk I shared with another man and landed on the two spare torpedoes on the deck. The engines were stopped, and we were ordered not to speak or move. The sub was now on an even keel, and there didn't seem to be anything seriously wrong. Later we were to learn that a British plane on anti-submarine patrol had sighted us from a distance, and dropped depth-charges over the spot where we had been. After lying motionless for about an hour the engines throbbed again, and we went on our way. One of the crew told me we were bound for Bordeaux.

The air was getting very foul, and we were told that as we wouldn't surface until after dark we must lie still and keep quiet, as the air was used up by unnecessary movement. We had a good meal of bread, cheese, and coffee during the afternoon, and then lay down to await night and fresh air. During the afternoon a voice speaking English came through the loudspeaker, saying that anyone caught touching any of the machinery would be thrown overboard. As I had no wish to stay longer in the submarine than I had to, I had no intention of doing it any damage. The order to keep still was very hard on me as my bladder was still very weak, so I asked one of the officers if I could speak to the commander. On explaining my predicament he took me amidships, and I had a talk with the commander. He was only about twenty-five, though he was the oldest member of the ship's company, and he, like the rest of the crew, had a beard. He spoke perfect English, and had a talk with me about the trip in the boat. He told me that as Bordeaux was blockaded by British planes he had decided to carry on to Saint-Nazaire, and we should be there in a couple of days. He said that as the midships portion of the submarine was too crowded to let me relieve myself he would give me a case of empty beer bottles to use.

We surfaced soon after this, and we could hear the mechanism of the sub working as we rose. After assuring themselves that the coast was clear the Germans opened up the conning-tower, and fresh air poured in. Air was pumped all through the vessel, and the diesel engine started up and kept going until nearly daybreak. The cook set his fire going, and made a hot meal for all hands, which he couldn't do when the sub was submerged. It was much more comfortable now with the fresh air, and everyone was happy and looking forward to going on shore. In the early morning we submerged again, and the submarine ran on batteries. It wasn't too bad, as occasionally, if the coast was clear, the commander would surface for short periods, and we could get fresh air.

About noon on the third day of January the warning bell went again, and the Germans dashed to their stations. I was lying alongside the spare torpedoes and quite close to the torpedo-tubes, and could watch the men waiting for orders. The sub would rise a few inches at a time, then submerge a bit, and it sounded just like being in a lift on shore. This went on for a while, and I asked one of the Germans what was going on. He said it was a British destroyer. You can imagine how I felt lying there and knowing we were stalking one of our own destroyers. Everything was deadly quiet, and then all of a sudden the alarm bell clanged out harshly. Immediately the nose of the sub went down at a terrific speed as she crash-dived. She seemed to be standing on her head. The suspense was terrible, and I could see that even the men standing by the torpedo-tubes were looking a bit drawn, as though waiting for something. Then came the first depth-charge, and the sub shook with the force of the explosion. We were still going down, but the angle was not so steep, and gradually the submarine came to an even keel. Then came the second and third explosions, and we were thrown all over the place. The sub seemed to jump and then rolled from side to side. The lights went out, and all the escape hatches were closed. She seemed to bump a bit a few seconds later, and I could only guess that we had hit the sea bottom. We could hear depth-charges going off, but they seemed to be farther away each time. There wasn't a sound now in our compartment, and I thought to myself that after coming through what I had I was to finish up like this, suffocating in a submarine at the bottom of the sea. A voice in the darkness told us to lie still and not move from where we were, which was rather hard to obey as we were all lying over each other. I lay across the spare torpedoes with a big German lying on my legs. Nobody in our compartment knew what damage had been done, but no water was coming in at our end. No orders were coming through, so we could only guess something had gone wrong amidships or aft. We lay for hours, the air getting foul, and drops of moisture falling on us from the deck head. I was choking and could hear the heavy breathing of others, and knew they were suffering as much as I was. The under-officer with us warned us not to speak or move as we would use up what air was left. I didn't think I should last long the way we were, and just lay feeling the drops of moisture dripping down in the darkness.

It seemed hours later when we heard a tapping from the other side of the bulkhead. Someone on our side tapped back an answer. They must have had some sort of code worked out beforehand, for the tapping went on for some time, until eventually the watertight door was opened, and one of the crew came through with a torch and some small square boxes which he placed on the deck. One of the men told me this was a way to test the condition of the air. I could hear a lot of hammering going on in the after section of the submarine, and a few men were working by torchlight on some mechanism in our compartment. It was early morning before the lights came on again, and the commander spoke through

C

the loudspeaker and told everyone to stay calm, and the damage to the after end would be repaired. We were all gasping for air, as the thirty-five extra men had used up the air sooner than would the normal crew.

The submarine got under way about daybreak and rose slowly to the surface. The hatches opened, and fresh air gushed in. We had no more incidents during the trip to Saint-Nazaire, which we reached about noon on the 4th of January. We slid slowly into the submarine pens, and the Germans all went ashore where a military band played on the quay and a number of high-ranking officers welcomed them. The remainder of us, all prisoners, stood on the deck watching everything, and wondering what was going to happen to us. Later in the afternoon I was taken on shore for interrogation, and then placed in a cell on my own. I remained there until the following day, when a guard came to take me to a truck bound for Nantes, and the train to Wilhelmshaven and captivity. I was sent to the Merchant Navy prison camp at Milag Nord, where I remained until the British Army arrived to free us in May 1945.

2 *Stern First*

SHALIMAR (F. C. HENDRY)

I

FOR nineteen days the large, iron, four-masted barque in which I was serving had been beating backwards and forwards, mostly under short canvas, across that abomination of desolation, the stormy tract of water that lies between Tierra del Fuego and the fringe of the Antarctic ice, trying to weather Cape Horn outward bound in the teeth of the great west wind, the driving squalls of sleet and snow, and the towering, rushing seas which surged continuously at her, exerting their terrific powers to drive her back to leeward and hinder her every attempt to make westing. On the evening of the nineteenth day, in a north-west gale, she was head-reaching to the south-west on the starboard tack with three lower topsails, foresail, and fore topmast staysail set—just as much canvas as she could stagger along under.

During the second dog-watch from six o'clock until eight, the starboard watch was on deck, and the four apprentices who were in it had been cowering miserably under the shelter of one of the boats on top of the after-house. This house, which was the half-deck and our home, stood on the maindeck between the break of the poop and the mizzen-mast, and was connected with the poop by a flying bridge. The apprentices were Tommy, who was a first voyager; Larry, a second voyager; George, who was in his third year; and myself, who had nearly finished my apprenticeship. Presently Tommy, who was keeping time, struck eight bells on the poop. It was repeated on the large bell on the forecastle-head. The two watches mustered aft and the starboard watch was ordered below, much to our relief, for we could see that the vessel was straining rather heavily, and we had feared that the foresail would have to be taken in by all hands at the change of the watch. Our luck was in, however, and, watching our chance, for the seas were breaking continuously over the weather rail and sweeping the main-deck, we eventually got the lee door of the half-deck open and all got safely inside. What a cheerless den it looked! A lamp, with the glass badly smoked on one side, hung from a beam, jerking to and fro in a drunken manner at its lanyard. Over a foot of water swished about the floor, welling up on the lee side so that the lower bunks were almost awash. The bread barge had been upset and spilt out the biscuits, which, sodden and pulpy, were washing about all over the place. Our sea-chests were lashed, but the lashings could not be got tight enough, so the chests slid backwards and forwards about six inches as the ship lurched violently to leeward and then back again. She was lying over at an angle that never got less than fifteen degrees from the perpendicular, and often reached thirty on the leeward roll.

Gloomily, we proceeded to take off our oilskins and seaboots, which was all the undressing we did down south there. In justice to ourselves, however, I must say that it usually took more than the ordinary vicissitudes of a Cape Horn passage to reduce us to this state of gloom. Only that morning, after an exhausting four hours on deck, we had gone below to a breakfast such as none of us would have placed before our dogs had we been at home, and yet the half-deck had rung with merry laughter. George, after suggesting that anyone who went to sea for a living when he could get a job ashore should have no difficulty whatever in qualifying for a lunatic asylum, and that he who went to sea for pleasure would go to hell for pastime, had rounded on Tommy and asserted it was well known that that youth —who had only turned sixteen—had been sent to sea because his mamma had discovered him making amorous overtures to the children's governess; and Tommy's spluttered, indignant denials and his girlish blushes had so convulsed us that our laughter was heard outside, and one of the watch on deck had risked the mate's displeasure and sneaked in to participate in the joke. Since then, however, something had happened. Jansen, a young Danish ableseaman, one of the smartest sailors in the ship, had gone overboard. All hands had been making fast the main upper topsail at eight bells in the afternoon watch, and Jansen, ignoring the old sailor's proverb of caution, "One hand for the owner and one for yourself," had let go the jackstay and was using both hands to haul the canvas on to the yard. The wind suddenly tore the canvas from his grasp. Clutching wildly at nothing he had fallen backward, hit the main yard-arm—for that yard was as usual braced up a little sharper than the topsail yards—as he dropped and had then fallen into the sea to leeward. With the exception of the mate, who was on top of the forward house, the captain, who was standing beside the man at the wheel, and Tommy, who was on the lee side of the poop, all hands were up on the yard. We knew, of course, that to lower a boat in that heavy sea was impossible, but all operations on the yard were suspended as we helplessly watched the yellow oilskin-clad figure floating aft. Tommy, with considerable presence of mind for a first voyager, whipped a coil of rope from a belaying-pin and threw it at Jansen, but the latter must have been stunned by his contact with the main yard and made no effort. Before he was twenty yards astern he had sunk like a stone.

We eventually got the topsail made fast and descended to the deck to find Tommy crying hysterically. Poor little devil! Six months before he had been at school and never witnessed a worse accident than a broken collar-bone at a Rugby match.

"If only there had been a boat-hook handy I might have had him," he wailed.

Jansen's death had profoundly impressed all hands—after all we were not a very large company—and at the moment they were probably as gloomy in the forecastle as we were in the half-deck. We crawled into our bunks and drew our sodden blankets over us. George, after wasting half a dozen matches, got the damp tobacco in his pipe to draw, and was noisily sucking at it. In an endeavour to dispel the gloom I spoke.

"Cheer up, chaps," I said; "it won't always be like this. Once we get a slant, ten days will take us up amongst the flying-fish again."

"Yes," George chimed in cheerfully; "and look here, Tommy, old man, although you *are* such an unspeakable rip, the first night we are in 'Frisco I'll take you up to Clark's in Kearny Street and give you the finest feed you ever had in your life."

"In the unlikely event of our ever getting to San Francisco," Larry began ponderously, "or indeed of ever getting anywhere beyond where we are now—"

"Oh, dry up, you lugubrious swine," George interrupted.

After that there was silence inside the half-deck, while outside the wind howled through the rigging and the great seas crashed on the deck and swirled around our little house. The weather seemed to me to be steadily getting worse.

"I hope we get our watch below," I remarked doubtfully. "That foresail will have to come in sooner or later."

There was no reply. I looked round the wretched hovel, which was dimly lit by the rays of the turned-down lamp. In the bunk beneath mine Tommy, fast asleep, was breathing peacefully. In the bunk opposite George was snoring; his pipe had fallen from his lips and was lying on his breast, but I had no anxiety because of that, for the damp tobacco would cease to smoulder as soon as he stopped sucking at it. For a few minutes I lay awake thinking. How much longer would this battle with the hostile elements and this acute discomfort—the wind, the cold, the pain on deck; the sopping misery of wet clothes and blankets below—continue? And would Jansen be the only sacrifice we would make to the insatiable greed of the Horn, or would others of us forget to keep one hand for ourselves and one for the owner and go the same way? Then I also fell asleep.

II

"Hey! *Hey!* HEY! you sleepers; show a leg; one bell."

I must have been asleep for nearly three and a half hours, but it only seemed like a minute since I closed my eyes when this ear-splitting yell echoed around the half-deck. In fine weather—in the Trades, for instance—we would take no notice of that first call further than turning over and going to sleep again; but off the Horn there was so much to do in the way of lashings round the wrists and ankles to keep the water from getting inside our oilskins, and "soul and body lashings" round our waists, that the quarter of an hour between one bell and eight bells was just sufficient, and we promptly sat up in our bunks. The small, blue-lipped apprentice from the port watch—clad in streaming yellow oilskins—who had called us, sat on one of the sea-chests and regarded us with cold disfavour.

"Oh, you pampered pets of the starboard watch," he said disgustedly.

"Hullo! what's the matter with *you*?" asked George, who had reached for his pipe—always his first action on being called.

"Matter!" he of the port watch replied bitterly. "It's all hands to take in the foresail at eight bells, and that's a good slice off our watch below gone."

"What's it like out there now?" I asked.

"Blowing like hell with squalls of sleet," was the reply. "That foresail is going to be a first-class frolic. The old man has hung on a bit too long this time."

He opened the lee door and vanished into the gloom. Silently we made our preparations, sitting up on the sea-chests so as to be clear of the swirling water, hauling on damp sea-boots and cold clammy oilskins, then fumbling with numb fingers at the rope-yarns with which we were lashing the latter. Eight bells struck, and with the last clang we cautiously opened the door and stepped out on to the main-deck into the darkness and

the shrieking gale. The second mate's voice came bellowing through the devilish screaming of the wind.

"Come on forward," he yelled. "All hands haul the
foresail up."

Just as we got to the fore part of the half-deck a huge
sea reared itself over the weather rail, and with one
accord we jumped for the mizzen fife-rail and held on.
The scene along the main-deck over which we had to
make our way, viewed from the fife-rail, was one that
might well have appalled the bravest amongst us. Although the vessel was lying over with her lee scuppers
under water, the seas were pouring in a continuous cas-
cade over the weather rail; and as if that were not
enough, she was scooping it in over the lee rail as well.
Evidently there were more ways of going overboard
than falling from aloft. Our captain had made himself
a reputation for weathering Cape Horn, and he went by
two golden rules. One was to get well to the southward
so as to be able to take advantage of the south-west wind
when it came—as come it must—and the other was to
keep the vessel moving; and we were carrying out both.
He hated heaving his vessel to; it seemed to him to be a
tame surrender this lying to, drifting dead to leeward
and losing all the westing he had made. Far better, he
declared, to keep head-reaching under all the canvas
she could carry and try to do something. Now, however,
the tumult which the elements had raised against him
had dismayed even his stout heart, and he *had* to shorten
sail. This time, undoubtedly, he had overdone it; as the
port watch apprentice said, he had hung on a bit too
long, and for once in a way the half-deck's criticism of
the cabin was correct.

The second mate, who was up on the fife-rail with
us, concealed behind a villainous squint and a voice like
an Atlantic liner's fog-horn one of the kindliest natures
I have ever known. Suddenly he turned to Tommy, who

was hanging on beside him, and roared—"What the hell are *you* doing here? Get up on the poop—this is no place for you. Come on the rest of you."

He leapt from the fife-rail, splashed through the water to the main-hatch, and we followed. Aided by the life-lines stretched along the deck fore and aft, we at last got forward to where all hands were gathered. It was impossible to distinguish them in the inky darkness, one could only tell them by the sound of their voices, and there were consequently many opportunities for skulking; in fact, we found out later that one of the able-seamen, a Dago, had taken no part in the proceedings at all, but had been lurking under the forecastle-head the whole time. Most of the men were cowed and dispirited by the hardships which we were enduring, but amongst them were some whom nothing could depress or dismay. At that time—about the end of last century—British ships were carrying many more foreigners in their forecastles than Britishers. The more respectable British seamen were finding plenty of employment in the great liners, and even in tramp steamers they were better paid and better fed than they were in wind-jammers, although there was a race of sailormen—alas! even then rapidly dying out—who would never go into steam. Unfortunately, they were generally the scum of the ports; hard-bitten, turbulent, and prone to getting drunk whenever they had the opportunity. In consequence, shipmasters much preferred the milder and more docile foreigners—mostly Dutchmen and Dagos—although most ships carried a few Britishers for just such occasions as this. We had three of them in the fore-castle—Liverpool Irishmen—and excellent seamen they were; but a more truculent, reckless, and foul-mouthed trio of hard cases and jail-birds never sailed the ocean. They had terrorised everyone in the forecastle, they were difficult to discipline, and they were generally detested, but there was not a man on board the ship from the captain downward who was not glad of their presence that night. It was said of them that they feared not God nor man—off the Horn we were to discover that they feared not the elements either. I do not remember their real names, but they were generally known as Dublin, Belfast, and Liverpool—the first two, probably, because they originally came from those ports, the latter because of his domicile. When we arrived we found that two of them were up on the gale-swept forecastle-head helping the Cockney boatswain to unhook the chain fore-tack, while the other was standing by in the seething lee scuppers ready to help the second mate to slack away the fore-sheet—about as dangerous and unpleasant a job as one could imagine.

The mate superintended the operations from the top of the forward house, and it was fortunate that he also possessed a voice like a fog-horn, for the cumulative effects of the various noises—the howling of the gale in the rigging, the thundering of the seas, the twanging of backstays, and the clanging of freeing-ports—was deafening.

"All ready?" he roared. "Slack away the sheet handsomely, mister. Haul away the lee clew garnet and the bunt-lines. Lively now."

The second mate and Belfast surged the sheet round the iron bitts, but the great sail, beginning to feel its freedom, defied for a time our every effort to haul it up. A number of the men seemed to be slacking, and only one of them—a Norwegian—could manage to sing out a mournful—

"Oh, ho! up mit her."

Suddenly a great wave towered to windward as high as the sheer-poles. The mate saw it coming, and yelled to us to hang on for our lives. We managed to get the bunt-lines and clew garnets belayed, and sprang to the

43

fife-rail and top of the house for safety; but how the
second mate and Belfast managed to get the sheet
secured round the bitts again and to avoid being
drowned down there to leeward I never knew. We began
hauling again, often up to our waists in the ice-cold
water and barely able to keep our feet on the greasy
rolling deck; but it was not until we were reinforced by
the boatswain and the three Irishmen that we got the
wind-filled monster into some sort of control. Eventually
we had done all we could do from the deck; bunt-lines
and leech-lines were as close up as we could get them,
but still the great sail above us was full of bags of wind
and slatting and thrashing with claps like thunder.

"Aloft and furl it," the mate roared.

"*Haloft and furl it.*" Dublin, repeating the order with
a prideful shout, was the first man to spring into the
weather rigging. We followed and, jambed hard against
the shrouds by the weight of the wind, slowly struggled
up the ratlines. On deck we had been drenched by
breaking seas and spray, now we were scourged by flying
hailstones. Eventually we reached the yard and laid out
on it, and the real fight with the foresail began. The
canvas was wet and heavy and ballooning out as stiff
as a board; the ship was lurching heavily, so that the
buckling steel yard swayed giddily in wide circles
through the air. Our only foothold was the wire foot-
rope stretched below the yard which swayed to and fro
as we worked, and the only grip for our half-frozen
fingers was the iron jackstay that ran along the top of
the yard and to which the sail was bent. In at the bunt,
where the work was heaviest, along with the second
mate and the boatswain, were the three Irishmen,
struggling like demons. They called the sail by an un-
printable name as they fought with it, they blasphemed
as long as they had breath, but inch by inch they
gathered up the stubborn folds. Once we almost had it

mastered; the weather leech had been passed along the yard, and some of the men were lying on it to keep it down. One or two of us sat down on the wire foot-ropes, hanging on with one hand to the stirrups and ready with the other to pass the gaskets which were to fasten the sail to the yard. Then a furious gust caught an open lug; some of the weaklings to windward let the leech go and the sail blew out free again, thrashing high above the heads of the men on the yard, who could do nothing but cling desperately to the jackstay, and nearly jerking those of us who were sitting on the foot-rope into eternity. Above me a Dutchman was sobbing with pain; the canvas had torn off two of his finger-nails. We had to watch our chance, wait for a lull, and start all over again. After another struggle we got the sail gathered up, and this time we managed to frap it to the yard with the gaskets. It was by no means a neat job—nothing like a harbour stow—but it was secure. We laid down from aloft, and as we reached the deck someone struck three bells—half-past one. The port watch was ordered below.

It was my wheel at two o'clock. I felt hungry, and remembering the state of our bread barge, I determined to go to the port forecastle, seeing that I was in the vicinity of it when I descended from the fore-yard, and borrow a couple of biscuits. Rather shyly, for I had never been in the forecastle at sea when it was occupied, I opened the door. The first thing that struck me was that the men were far more comfortable when below than we were; there was no water swishing about their floor, and they had a lighted bogey stove, round which there hung a number of weird-looking garments. Some of the men of the watch below were already in their bunks, others were sitting on their sea-chests. The atmosphere was thick; and but one of the men were smoking, and the stove was smoking too. Near the door, with one hand to his face, which was streaming with blood, cowered one of the Dagos. As I entered he addressed me.

"He puncha me on da nose. He puncha me on da nose," he whimpered, indicating Liverpool with his other hand.

Liverpool took two steps forward in the jaunty manner peculiar to various hooligans and Apaches and stuck out his lower jaw.

"If ye don't git to hell out o' this, ye white-livered spawn of an ice-cream barrow," he snarled, "I'll kicka yer ribs in as well."

"Where me go?" wailed the unfortunate Dago. "Me no posseebly stoppa da deck."

"Go!" replied Liverpool with a bitter sneer. "Go to the hole that ye was hidin' in while *we* was makin' the fores'l fast."

III

At four bells I relieved the man at the wheel. With the foresail off her the ship was certainly going along a little easier, but the weather was, if possible, getting worse; squall succeeded squall in rapid succession; the clouds seemed to be denser; the darkness was more overwhelming and broken only by an occasional phosphorescent gleam on the foaming crest of an approaching wave. Because of the blinding snow accompanying the squalls I could rarely see the nearest of the sails that were set—the mizzen lower topsail—and had to judge how close the vessel was to the wind by the feel of it. She was carrying the helm about half down, and I seldom had to move the wheel; indeed, I could almost have gone to sleep at it but for the fact that occasionally a sea would strike the rudder and start the wheel spinning so that it nearly tore the arms out of me, and once or twice almost flung me over the top of it. It was a dreary, monotonous business, and I fervently looked forward to the end of the watch as, with the collar of my oilskin coat pulled well up and my sou'wester well down, I leant against the north-west gale, my head half-turned away from it, watching for the arm-jarring jolts of the wheel and noting the passing of the time by the too infrequent striking of the bell.

A tarpaulin had been lashed in the weather jigger rigging, and under it the captain and the second mate were sheltering. At intervals the latter would stagger aft to the lighted binnacle to see how the ship was heading, otherwise I was left to my own devices. About a quarter past three the wind lulled a little, the snow ceased, and both of them came along to the binnacle. The captain seemed to be restless and anxious; he looked round the horizon, then went below into the cabin. When he returned to the poop he had another look at the compass card in the binnacle, another long stare at the horizon, particularly to windward and right ahead, as if he were trying to read something there; then he spoke to the second mate.

"I don't like the look of it, mister," he said. "We ought to be on the other tack, you know. We will wear her round at eight bells."

My heart sank. That meant a good slice off *our* watch below; in fact, it meant an extra hour at the wheel for me. The wind lulled still more, and after another pro-longed stare ahead the old man again sought the cabin.

"I like the look of it less than ever, mister," he said when he returned. "The glass has stopped falling; it looks like a shift of wind, and we're on the wrong tack for it. The sooner it's eight bells the better."

His remarks call for a little explanation. The long-drawn-out gales of the southern hemisphere, such as the one we were experiencing, usually begin with the wind

47

from the north, backing to the north-west. It remains in that direction for some time, gradually increasing in strength, with a falling barometer and rain or snow. Then the barometer ceases to fall, and shortly afterwards, with little other warning than a clearing of the weather, the wind flies into the south-west and for a time blows harder than ever, the shift of wind being followed by a rapid rise of the glass. It follows, therefore, that to avoid being caught aback, the vessel just before the shift of wind should be on the port tack, so that the wind will shift aft. We were on the starboard tack, so that the shift would bring the wind from almost dead ahead. When a square-rigged vessel is caught aback—that is, with the wind blowing on the wrong side of her sails—she is in about as bad a predicament as she could well be ; if she is carrying a press of canvas she will probably be dismasted, while even under short canvas as we were at that time, with the heavy sea that was running anything might happen.

For a few moments the old man fidgeted about, then his anxiety seemed to get the better of his consideration for the slumbering watch below.

"Strike one bell now, mister, and call the watch," he ordered.

The bell was struck; the second mate left the poop to gather together the men of his watch and to make preparations for the operation of wearing ship. Then suddenly the weight seemed to go out of the wind altogether, and the ship came almost on an even keel; the comparative silence was startling. Heavy rain began to fall. As if petrified the captain stared out on the lee bow, where, following his gaze, I could see a clearing low down in the sky. He quickly pulled himself together.

"Hard up the helm," he shouted to me.

Then he ran forward to the break of the poop, and as I spun the wheel round I could hear him roaring—

"Square the cro'jack yard. All hands on deck."

By this time it was almost a dead calm, the sails were slatting against the masts and the ship had not sufficient headway on her to enable her to answer her helm. She lay almost stopped and helpless, the waves breaking over her, or flinging her about, just as they wished. The clearing in the sky to the south-west grew and spread; its upper part seemed to be fringed with black clouds, which it was chasing before it, and from which large jagged masses tore themselves and seemed to come hurtling straight at the ship. Below on the main-deck I could hear ropes running through sheaves and the shouts of the watch on deck, who were struggling with the crossjack yard; then those sounds were abruptly drowned as with a roar the wind struck the vessel two points on the port bow. It was a wild moment; sea and sky seemed to be mixed in one awful smother. The ship gathered sternway, which increased rapidly, and presently everything—sky, sea, and ship—seemed to be rushing straight at me where I stood right aft; it was a weird and terrifying spectacle. The captain, who had come aft again, silently helped me to put the wheel amidships—had we put it over one way or the other it would have meant a smashed rudder—then he stood beside me, hanging on to the wheel as if he was paralysed. The ship was now pitching heavily.

A heavier gust than ever crashed at us from almost dead ahead; the clouds had passed away and it came from a clear sky. The great vessel's bow rising from a plunge appeared to hang for a moment, then instead of dipping down again it seemed to rise in the air. Higher and higher it rose, I looked fearfully behind me; the water was bubbling up over the half-round on to the poop and was nearly up to the wheel grating. Absolutely shaken and unnerved the old man let go the wheel, made a gesture of despair, and clutched with both hands at

D

the sou'wester on his head; then he turned to me, and in a voice that I could hardly recognise because of the tremble that was in it, he shouted—

"My God! she's foundering! She's going down by the stern!"

Although my instinct was to get forward away from that icy black water which was now almost up to my feet, I hung on to the wheel in a helpless agony of mind. My first thought was for my shipmates struggling down there on the main-deck; but what could I do? What good would a warning be to them? Certainly the old man and myself would be the first to be engulfed, but in less than five minutes there would be no place of safety on board, not even the main truck; everything would have disappeared beneath the waves.

Bang! Bang!

Above the din and the roar of the wind there came two reports exactly like those produced by the firing of a section of field-guns. The great vessel's bow wavered and began to settle down again; very slowly at first, then with a violent sickening plunge into the trough of the head sea. We peered anxiously forward, wondering what had happened and what her next move would be; then we became aware of a small figure crawling along the poop towards us and clinging on to the skylight bars as it came.

"Fore and main topsails blown away, sir," the owner of it shouted, his shrill voice carrying well through the gale.

I recognised the voice as Tommy's. Even as he screamed out his information, I had become aware that there was something wanting aloft; where the black strips of the fore and main lower topsails had been there was now a strange emptiness. The old man straightened himself up and the old ring of confidence

50

had returned to his voice when he answered Tommy with the conventional—

"All right."

Then he turned to me.

"Thank God for that," he shouted.

IV

Before long the vessel's bow began to swing rapidly to starboard; the fore topmast staysail of stout No. o storm canvas had stood, and was paying her head off the right way. The crowd down on the main-deck by almost superhuman efforts had got the yards on the mizzen-mast round, and the mizzen lower topsail filling, the ship gathered headway again and began to fly through the water. I had crossed to the other side of the wheel and the old man had helped me to put the helm hard down, but for a time the ship was unmanageable and refused to look at her rudder. Although the wind had shifted, the sea was still running from the old direction and was nearly dead ahead, so that the ship was pitching her bows clean under and was threatening to bury herself. The seas were sweeping the main-deck fore and aft. Eventually the rudder had its effect; the ship came up to the wind again and presently lay hove-to on the port tack and comparatively safe.

Although the snow had ceased and it was now clear, it was colder than ever, for the wind was blowing straight up from the Antarctic. The captain went below and I was left alone on the poop hanging on to the jolting wheel. I had little hope of relief for some time; the yards on the fore and main masts had yet to be hauled round, although there were no sails set on them, and I knew that things on the main-deck would be in a frightful state of chaos and that the watch would not be ordered below until everything had been cleared up.

Braces would be out through the freeing-ports, jammed under the spare spars, or entwined round the bulwark stanchions, and all hands would be diving for them in the icy water, for all the gear would have to be stopped up in the rigging ready to be flung on the deck clear for running in case of an emergency. The time wore on slowly. Dawn started to creep in, and as it grew brighter objects aloft began to shape themselves out of the gloom ; first the mizzen lower topsail, a narrow strip of canvas, sodden and black, straining furiously at the buckling yard to which it was bent; then I made out the main and fore masts with a host of small, ragged, fluttering pennons where the fore and main lower topsails had been. Farther forward the fore topmast staysail stood out nobly, but, for all that, the tall clipper looked very bare, draggled and forlorn, leaning over with no canvas set on three out of her four lofty masts. The waves seemed to be getting slightly smaller and were now running true with the wind, but occasionally one would mount, burst, and fill the main-deck green. The sky had turned a dull steely grey, and down on the lee quarter a few streaks of red gave promise that the sun, which we had not seen for days, would soon be rising.

I could see very few of the men about the deck, but, from their shouts, I knew that all hands were still working like beavers. I began to long for relief, for I was cold and tired and cramped. To my disappointment the galley funnel showed no sign of smoke; not that it mattered to me at the moment, for the watch which was going below would get no coffee in any case, but I knew that the fire had been washed out the night before, and I was speculating on the chance of getting something hot for breakfast later on. At last from underneath the break of the poop I heard the mate's voice and knew that the time of my relief was not very far distant.

"That'll do, the watch," he shouted.

Then came another order—the most pleasant one the windjammer sailor ever heard off Cape Horn.

"Grog-oh!"

After our night of hardship we were going to be heartened by a tot of rum. I could picture the group of sodden, bruised, and miserable wretches clustering round the open pantry hatch which was let into the break of the poop, waiting for the steward to hand out the strong liquor which would introduce a momentary glow of comfort into their frozen bodies, but not a soul could I see from my position at the wheel. After about five minutes Liverpool mounted the lee side of the poop and came along it with jaunty step to relieve me. He crossed over to windward and, taking advantage of the fact that there was no officer in sight, he stood in front of me instead of relieving the wheel in his usual sea-manlike manner and, smacking his lips, he said—

"Smell me breath."

I could without undue effort.

"You surely have more than your whack there," I said.

"I have," he replied; "I have two whacks."

"How did you manage that?"

"Well, ye see, when the stooard starts to ladle out the grog, I lines up amongst the very first and has me tot. Then I hangs on for a bit an' by-an'-by Antonio comes along. 'Stooard,' I ses, glarin' at Antonio an' at the same time showin' him me fist in a business-like way, 'Antonio has come aft to say as how he don't want his tot an' I can have it.' 'Is that so, Antonio?' says the stooard, an' Antonio not bein' too keen on another 'punch on da nose,' nods his head an' I drinks his grog. Sure it's a fine mornin'."

"I'm glad you like it," I said without enthusiasm.

"Well, here you are. By the wind—she's carrying the helm nearly hard down."

Liverpool bit a chew off a plug of tobacco, squared his shoulders, and seized the spokes.

"By the wind it is," he said. "An' ye had better hurry up or ye'll be losin' *your* whack too."

I was just in time; the steward was closing the pantry hatch, having served the last of the men. I was chilled to the very marrow of my bones; never have I wanted a stimulant more or relished it better, and the strong sweet liquor almost made me into a new man as I splashed along to the half-deck. It looked much the same as it had done when we left it at midnight except that various articles, such as socks, which had been missing for days and had evidently been reposing under the lower bunks on the port side, had washed out from their hiding-places now that the ship was leaning over the other way and were lying in the middle of the floor. Larry and Tommy, not wanting grog, had come straight below and were asleep in their bunks; the former, who had a blood-stained bandage round his head—for he had been damaged in a collision with a bulwark stanchion—was moaning fitfully in his sleep. George, with a haggard face grimed with salt spray and dazed bloodshot eyes, evidently about all in, was sitting on his seachest puffing at his pipe. As with dirty fingers, blue with cold, I fumbled at the buttons of my oilskins, we discussed the events of the night. As I could well imagine they had a terrible time down on the main-deck, up to their necks at times in the rushing water. There had been many narrow escapes from drowning, but when I mentioned the greatest escape of all, George looked at me in blank amazement and could not take it in. Indeed, I rather think, despite the fact that I was senior to him, he would have called me a liar, only I happened to be slightly bigger and much handier with my fists than he was. It was now about six o'clock, and we would be called again at twenty past seven, so without further argument I clambered into my bunk and settled myself down amongst the wet blankets.

For almost the first time since I had been at sea sleep refused to come. My muscles began to bunch under the skin with cramp, but even after I had got them soothed, sleep failed me; my brain was busy, actively thinking over the events of the night. At last, about seven o'clock, I dozed off and commenced to dream. I was again at the wheel, and once more the ship's head began to lift. Higher and higher it rose until the ship was almost perpendicular and about to fall over on top of me; then I sat up in my bunk sweating with fright, just as seven bells went and the apprentice from the other watch came in to call us. His news was not too bad. The sea had moderated still more, and the deck was much drier, although it was still blowing pretty hard and was bitterly cold.

Presently I heard the tramp of feet on the deck. The watch on deck had got another main lower topsail out of the sail locker and were about to bend it. They had taken the gantline to one of the capstans and were heaving the sail up abaft the mast. One of them struck up the verse of a chanty—by his voice I recognised that the soloist was Belfast. Timed by the metallic clink of the capstan pawls, and accompanied by the humming of the wind in the rigging, the chorus swelled into a triumphant roar, then died away in a mournful cadence:

"Blow, boys, blow,
For Cal-i-for-ni-o;
There's plenty of gold, so I've been told,
On the banks of the Sacramento."

V

During our next watch below I again mentioned the narrow escape which the ship had had, but met with the same reception; indeed George, reinforced by the others, openly scoffed at me, with the result that I never spoke about it again, but waited my time, confident that the two mates would be sure to refer to it before long and thus confound the scoffers. They did not, however, and I did not care to mentioned it to them for fear that *they* might laugh at me. The captain was, of course, unapproachable as far as I was concerned. In puzzling the thing out, I came to the conclusion that all hands fighting for their lives down there on the flooded main-deck had been too much absorbed in their own troubles to notice anything out of the way, and besides, it was only a person standing right aft—as the captain and I had been—or right forward who would have got a clear view of what happened. There had been no one right forward. The look-out man could not possibly have remained on the forecastle-head that night—he would have been washed off it—and indeed, there had been no one on the look-out at all, for our vessel was so helpless that even had another ship been reported we could have done nothing to get out of her way. At times I even wondered if I had been mistaken as to the danger or if I had magnified it. But no! There was not only the evidence of my eyes but also of my ears. There could have been no mistaking the bitter wail of the momentarily broken man who had stood watching in helpless suspense his vessel—the precious charge committed to his care—foundering with all hands under his feet. Although I kept my ears well open, I never once heard the incident referred to during the remainder of the voyage; indeed, a good many years elapsed before I again had a chance to discuss it.

In May 1916, just after Kut fell, I, in common with a good many other officers of the original I.E.F. 'D' who had not been captured, got a month's leave in India. I spent my leave at a hill station, and at the end of it returned to Bombay and there embarked on a hired transport—a very fine steamer—bound for Basra, where I was to rejoin my regiment. The transport, which was absolutely packed with officers and other ranks, sailed at noon, and about six o'clock in the evening a small gang of officers, of whom I was one, was hanging about the smoking-room door rather impatiently waiting for the sun to touch the horizon. Presently I saw, stuck up inside the smoking-room, a list of boat stations for the crew. I stepped inside and idly surveyed it, then suddenly noticed that the signature of the master at the bottom of it was familiar. Unless I was greatly mistaken, it was the signature that was on my indentures—that of my old skipper. I walked along forward hoping to get a glimpse of him on the bridge, but just before I got to it he emerged from his cabin and mounted the bridge ladder. Without doubt it was he. His closely trimmed brown beard was now completely grey; instead of the long black oilskin coat and sou'wester with which I was so familiar, or the light tussore silk coat and soft felt hat that he used to wear in the tropics, he was now clad in spotless white with glittering shoulder straps, and the peak of his badge cap was heavy with gold braid; but there was no mistaking his broad sturdy figure. I did not care to disturb him just then, for he was obviously busy, so, the sun having set, I hastened back to the smoking-room intent on other business.

When I left the saloon after dinner he was still at his table, and I waited outside in the lounge for him. When he came out of the saloon he was accompanied by a general, with whom he stood talking. On principle I avoided generals, so I waited until the skipper went on deck, when I followed him and made myself known. Five minutes afterwards I was seated in his cabin, where even generals hesitated to intrude. What is more, I was invited to make it my home for the rest of the trip, and having been a sailor, I had even been made free of that sacred edifice, the bridge. I felt that I was in for a good trip. Before long the skipper was calling me by my Christian name, and I was sirring him as if it were only yesterday, instead of nearly twenty years ago, that we had sailed together.

"Well, well," said the old man as he beamed at me, "I like to keep trace of all my old boys, but you had eluded me altogether. I never thought of looking in the Indian Army List for you." He glanced at one of my shoulder-straps. "Nor did I expect that one of my apprentices would turn into a Rajput."

Many a boy had passed through the captain's hands in his old sailing-ship days, and most of them had been a credit to him. A few had been drowned, but most of them were now officers in fine steamers—some actually in command—and nothing gave him greater pleasure than to have one of them come up to him in a shipping office or at his agents and say, "Don't you remember me, Sir?" We yarned away about old times and old shipmates. I was not the only one of our batch who had "swallowed the anchor". Tommy had only half-swallowed it; he was in the Bengal Pilot Service and doing well; the captain had seen him quite recently. But Larry, the lugubrious, had gone the whole hog, and was now a Methodist parson somewhere in the Midlands; while George—well, I gathered from the old man that, in his opinion, George had done better than any of us. He was starring in musical comedy. The last time the old man had been in London he sat in the stalls of a West End theatre and recognised George on the stage. After the show was over he went round to the stage-door and sent in his card. George came down, fell on his neck, and afterwards gave him the time of his life. I determined that I also would call on George if ever I returned to Town. Presently the old man sat back in his chair and a mischievous twinkle came into his blue eyes.

"Do you remember the time I caught you down the sugar cask?" he asked solemnly.

Did I remember it? Was I ever likely to forget it? It happened during my very first voyage to sea, when I was a very small nipper indeed. At the time the food on board was scarce and rather bad, and a state of war existed between the brightest brains of the half-deck and the rather dull-witted Scotch steward. The latter's life was one of perpetual worry; neither the pantry nor storeroom which he controlled were safe from our depredations, and the culminating point in the war came when a bottled-gooseberry tart which had been made for the cabin Sunday dinner was spirited away from the galley, the attention of the cook having been successfully attracted elsewhere. After that the steward invoked the all-powerful assistance of the captain, who mustered us all in the cabin and lectured us all severely.

"You won't get to windward of *me*," he stormed. "I know all your tricks—done 'em all myself—and the first one of you that I catch stealing gets a good rope's ending."

For a time this warning, if it did not entirely suspend operations, at least curtailed them. Then, one unfortunate day, I was sent down into the lazarette—the large storeroom beneath the cabin, which was entered through a hatch in the cabin floor—to do some job for the steward. Shortly after we had gone down the steward left me, and remembering the presence of a cask of loaf sugar which I had paid attention to on a previous occasion, I crawled across some intervening cases and bags amongst which it was wedged, with the intention of having another go at it. I found it nearly empty, but managed to get out and eat a few lumps before I returned to my job. Then my conscience smote me—not for what I had done, but because I had forgotten my shipmates. I crawled back to the cask with the intention of securing a few lumps for them, and was well into it, head first and feet in the air, scraping around the bottom, when I heard a noise which indicated that the steward was returning. In an endeavour to make a quick exit from the cask my hands slipped and I dropped on to my elbows, my further struggles only wedging me into the cask more firmly. The old steward approached, then I heard his voice; he seemed to take in the situation at a glance.

"Imph'm! Ay, ay, och ay!" he said.

Without another word he left the lazarette and went up into the cabin. Still struggling to get out, I realised what he had gone for, and my surmise proved only too correct. Very shortly afterwards I heard two men coming down the ladder, then I heard the captain's voice.

"Oh, very nice," he said ironically. "Steward, bring me a short length of ratline line."

I heard the steward depart. In the presence of the captain I had, of course, ceased to struggle. Presently the steward returned, and I presume that he handed the captain the length of ratline. I was certainly in the very best position possible for receiving what was coming to me—but that will be about enough of *that*.

I determined to make a counter-attack.

"Do *you* remember," I said, "that time off the Horn when we were caught aback under three lower topsails and nearly lost her?"

To my discomfiture the captain regarded me with a vacant stare as if he did not know what I was talking about. For quite half a minute we sat in silence looking at each other, I rather sorry that I had spoken, while he, as it turned out, was bluffing. Then a gleam of comprehension—almost, I thought, of relief—came into his eyes.

"Of course," he said, "I had forgotten. You were at the wheel."

He nodded his head gravely, and then continued—

"I expect you have been pretty near death a few times during this war," he said, "but you were never nearer to it than you were that night. If those topsails hadn't blown away—"

He stopped abruptly and jerked his forefinger down towards the deck.

"Yes," he went on, "in less than five minutes she would have gone right under and sunk like a stone. More than that, I am perfectly convinced after what I saw that night that many a fine ship that was eventually posted as missing at Lloyd's after attempting a Cape Horn passage was lost the same way; and a damned silly way of losing a ship it was when you come to think of it. Well, well! I haven't discussed that business with a soul from that day to this."

"I tried hard to discuss it with the others in the half-deck, Sir, but they laughed at me."

"Ah," he replied, "I was wiser than you. I realised at once that you and I were the only two on board who were likely to have noticed what had happened, so I lay low and said nothing. Why should I? I had committed a grave error of judgment in keeping her so long on the starboard tack and I certainly didn't want my name to be bandied about the seven seas as the man who nearly lost his ship because he was too soft-hearted to call the watch below. The next morning the mates sympathised with me because we had lost the topsails. I laughed it off—told them we would get new ones out of the insurance. As for the men, few of them would imagine that anything out of the way had happened; I expect some of them would think it was a new way of getting the ship on to the other tack. But, by heavens! that was a wild night. *I* never want to see Cape Horn again. Hullo! five bells already—half-past ten. Go on, Rajput; it's time you were in bed."

3 *Life-Story of a Schooner*

WESTON MARTYR

I WISH Old Man Destiny would give me an opportunity of starting my life all over again. He seems
fond of playing his little games with me, and I
want a chance to get a little of my own back. I should
like the Old Gentleman to have me washed overboard
in a typhoon, or he might arrange a vicious weather roll
and jerk me off the main top-gallant lee yard-arm so
that I landed on my back across the mizzen fife-rail. I
am not very particular how he finishes me, but I should
prefer one of those sure or sudden and not too messy
endings which, from time to time, I have watched the
Old Boy stage so perfectly. Then, when I was feeling
comfortably at rest at last, I *know* Mr. Destiny would
come ambling along. He would be grinning, I expect,
and he would pick out my most fractured rib and kick
it. Having thus attracted my attention, he would say,
"Aha! my lad. You lie there smiling, do you? You think
you've escaped from life at last. No more worry or work
or pain; what? You think that's all done with, don't
you? Well, my boy, it isn't, so don't flatter yourself, for
I'm going to send you back to life again! Ah! I *thought*
that would make you sit up. And, *this* time, so that you
may properly appreciate what an ass you are, I'm going
to let you choose your own job in the world. Now, hurry
up, for I've got a lot of other fools to attend to this
morning. Choose! What shall it be? King? Emperor?
Millionaire? Illustrious author?—or any other foolish-

63

ness you like. Choose!" And then I would answer quickly, before he could change his mind. "I'll be a boat-builder," I'd cry. "I'll make ships out of wood; and this time I'll enjoy life and be happy. And I've fooled you for once, Mr. William Destiny, or whatever your name is." And then, if the old gent stuck to his promise (he probably wouldn't), I should come back here—and have a good time.

Of all the different materials in this world that man can shape and fashion and mould, give me wood to work on. It is such kindly stuff, most of it, and one can see at once, the result of any effort spent upon it. Consider, for instance, the difference there is between gently planing clean and curly shavings from a piece of sweetly smelling pine-wood, and arduously and brutally filing minute bits of dirty metal from a bar of intractable incompliant steel. And, personally, I would rather be able, say, to fay the knee-of-the-head upon a stem than formulate new philosophies. To "fay" is, in the language of the dictionaries, "to join one piece of timber so closely to another that there shall be no perceptible space between them." And as I watched Old John expertly faying the *Southseaman*'s stem to her keel, I thought to myself that he was making a better job of his work than most philosophers make of theirs. For there were never any "perceptible spaces" in Old John's work. You could not see through it anywhere.

The job Old John had in hand at the moment was to join together the ends of two 7in. $\times$ 7in. oak timbers. One piece was long and straight, and the other long and curved, and they were both extremely hard and heavy and troublesome to handle; and they had to be so strictly and faithfully married that nothing could part them in this world short of a power that would shatter the keel itself. For building a ship is not like building a house. In a house, if one thing is fastened on top of another so that it will not fall, all will be well enough; but the joints of a ship are going to be pulled and wrenched and strained and twisted and worried at all her life through, so they have to be made to *hold*.

And here I want to tell you a story about a ship that was made during the war. She was a steamer, and she was built of wood—good wood; and the men who designed and made her were good and able craftsmen too. As soon as this ship was completed she steamed a few miles down a river and commenced to load a full cargo of coal. For at that time ships were being murdered at sea by the dozen each day, and the coal was worth its weight in copper on the other side of the ocean. When the ship felt the first weight of her cargo she began to squeak, and then she cried out in pain. But the coal, as I have said, was badly wanted, so the stevedores, and even the ship's own men, pretended not to hear the ship's complaint, but just went ahead trimming in the cargo through four hatches at the rate of 200 tons an hour. And when a thousand tons or so were lying heavy within her the ship stopped crying out aloud, for by then she was in so much pain that she could only groan. She groaned dreadfully, though, for I heard her myself and she frightened me—and this is a true tale.

But the men still went ahead loading the coal, until, with only 300 tons more needed to bring her down to her marks, the poor ship gave such a sudden loud scream that the master stevedore jumped and turned pale, and blew his whistle to stop all work at once. For a while he scratched his head and looked troubled as he spat reflectively down the main hatch. Then, "There's a war on," said he, "so we've got to give her the rest, I guess. We're breaking her heart, though, poor thing; but it's her back we'll break if we ain't careful. Put the hatches on Nos. 1 and 4, boys, and we'll try and finish her off amidships. And if she won't take it all, there, we'll leave it—for I'd sooner get fired than break a ship in half!"

So they finished her off amidships, and sent her out to sea.

It was a fine day, calm and hazy, as she steamed out into deep water, and she moved now without a sound, as if her teeth were clenched—and she trembled. She went along like a man who carries too heavy a burden, and presently she tripped and stumbled (it was only a little ground swell)—and she opened out and fell apart like a flimsy old crate that someone had stepped on. In five seconds there was nothing there at all except a floating scum of coal dust, with some timbers and an odd man or two bobbing about in the middle of it.

This is a true story; but the point I want you to notice is that this ship was made by carpenters: house carpenters—shore carpenters; and she was not built by shipwrights at all.

As I watched Old John slowly and carefully ruling his bevellings on the fore-end of the *Southseaman's* keel, I thought of the ship the carpenters had made, and I felt glad Old John had been working for fifty years or so at the shipwright's trade.

Old John at work was an interesting and instructive spectacle. He was so very delicate and careful that if you watched him for only a little while you might think him slow; but, in spite of the apparent leisureliness of his methods, the amount of work he managed to get through in a day was extraordinary. I watched him do his first day's work upon the schooner, and at the end of it I had learnt another lesson, for he showed me there is an attitude of mind which, if adopted before one sets out to accomplish any task, can save one a world of worry and trouble; and these are two abominable things which I have always been most anxious to avoid.

The various timbers which were to form the schooner's

66

backbone had been selected by Tom and MacAlpin, and then sawn to their approximate dimensions in Mac-Alpin's mill and carted to the building shed. And here I find myself wanting to tell you about MacAlpin, and how he selected those timbers and what he said while he was doing it; but Old John has got on to the stage first, so we had better stick to him in case I become too much confused in the telling of this tale. Imagine Old John, therefore, arriving at the shed in the morning and preparing to start upon his day's work. He carries with him a large and flattish box in which are the tools of his trade. He takes off his coat, and then examines the pile of rough-sawn timbers on the floor—the disarticulated joints of the schooner's backbone—which it is his job to join into one solid and united whole. This appears to me to be a daunting and practically impossible task, for there are many timbers of various sizes and shape, and they are all covered with a maze of mystical lines and marks where Tom has been busy measuring.

Here is a list of the timbers Old John has to shape and eventually join together: the stem, apron, stemson, gripe, keel, lower keel, false keel, keelson, rider-keelson, deadwood (three timbers), sternson, inner post, and stern post. But the sight of all this does not daunt Old John. Directing his two helpers to sort out the keelson and its members and pile them on one side for future attention, John proceeds to feel the edge of all his tools, and then slowly and carefully to sharpen one or two of them on his oilstone. And while he is doing this let me seize my chance and explain why there are going to be so many parts in the *Southseaman*'s spine. We had decided, Tom and George and I, after much deliberation, that the schooner should be built in the old-fashioned way. It was the way they always had built boats in Sheldon for one thing, and, for another, we liked the idea. As Tom pointed out, it is not so much the actual strength of the timber one builds into a ship as the tenacity of her fastenings which makes for security and durability, and the old method of fastening and reinforcing all joints appealed to George and me; and we thought then, and I still think now, that it is superior to the modern practice. In thinking this I may be quite mistaken; but Tom's way sounded and looked good to us—so we decided to adopt it. This business of reinforcing the joints Old John called "succouring the scarphs," and I think it was this perfect and illuminating phrase which made me decide at once that all the *Southseaman's* scarphs must undoubtedly be succoured.

This will account for the number of parts that Old John had to join together; because the stemson, for instance, succours the scarphs of the apron, as the apron does those of the stem. It is true that we thus had to employ three separate timbers where one, or at most two, are used to-day; but, owing to the increased strength we were able to secure by our extra fastenings and succourings, we could afford to cut down the scantlings considerably and thus actually save a little weight. You will consider our keel too light, maybe, but succoured as it was by the lower keel, keelson, and rider-keelson, it made a stronger foundation for the boat than is to be found in most yachts today.

When Old John was quite satisfied with the condition of his tools, he had the timber which was to form the main keel raised up on chocks a few inches, and then he sat astride one end of it, smelt it, stroked it with his fingers, and minutely examined its texture and its grain. " 'Twill do," said he, " 'tis a good piece o' heart wood, well seasoned, and no druxey dry-rot'll ever touch this one. But we'll turn her over, lads, and work on t'other side, for the grain ain't just right for an under bevelling here where Tom's marked her. Ease her round, my sons, a half turn; and you, Jim, start on the scarph at the other end. And, Andrew, you tell Tom what I'm agoing to do."

You will notice here that the manager's dispositions are altered by the workman, and that the manager is duly advised of the change it is proposed to make. This sort of thing happened fairly frequently while the schooner was being built, and at first sight it might appear that such unconventional proceedings were likely to produce confusion and, perhaps, chaos in the conduct of the work. But, as a matter of fact, such was far from being the case; and, indeed, I think that this is one of the reasons why the work turned out by the old-fashioned Sheldon methods was so much superior to anything I have seen produced by a modern machine-ridden yard. Tom Brough was just as good a craftsman as the men who, nominally, worked under him, and he was a more efficient organiser than any of them. But every now and then, of course, some point or other would escape Tom's eagle eye, and in a modern plant a point overlooked by the directing staff is usually a point lost for good. But in Sheldon, if Tom missed anything, somebody else would surely notice it, *and* attend to it—when all would be well. And there is another point concerning this independent Sheldon habit which must be borne in mind, and this is illustrated by the fact that, although Old John had quite made up his mind to work on the opposite side of the keel to that marked out by Tom, yet he waited until Tom appeared and approved the change before actually commencing to cut that scarph. All this explanation must, I fear, be very tedious for you; but I am anxious to make clear the spirit which lay behind the work in that old-fashioned shipyard, for, alas! it is only very rarely that one may meet with that same spirit today.

Old John, it seemed to me, took a long while getting to work, for Jim at the other end of the keel had been busy with a mallet and chisel for some minutes before John made his first deliberate cut. Jim was one of those quick impatient workers, and he hammered and pried and made the chips fly so fast that I could see he would finish his end before Old John had his scarph half done. But after a while I began to notice there was method in the slow and careful preparations Old John had made. When Jim wanted a gouge he had to get up and fetch it, while John had all the tools he needed placed handily by his side. Then the hardness of the oak appeared to bother Jim, for from time to time he found it necessary to jump up and sharpen his chisels on the stone. There was a deal of fuss and hustle all the time at Jim's end of the log, but at John's end things were very peaceful and quiet. And once Old John sat down and got to work he never stopped at all until the job was done. So, in the end, he finished before Jim, without hurrying himself, and, what is more, he produced a very beautiful piece of work. As I bent down to admire it, I told John how he had surprised me by finishing before Jim; and at that the old man turned round to look at Jim, who was still hard at it. "Yes, Jim's all right," said he; "but he's young yet, and his trouble is he had that job all done, in his mind, before he'd rightly started in on it. So now, o' course, he's all of a sweat. Now, ye can't worry *and* work fast, d'ye see?"

The scarph in a keel usually looks something like this:—

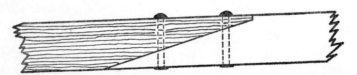

But this simple joint did not suit Old John at all, so he married his timbers together and dovetailed them in such a way that they would hold without any bolts if need be. So where the timbers joined in the *Southsea-man*'s hull they looked rather like this:—

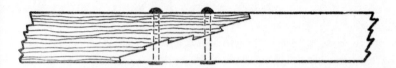

To join these two pieces you have to slide the tenons sideways into the mortises, and work such as this has perforce to be perfectly done, for if it is not the timbers refuse to slide together at all. During his first day's work I watched Old John make four of these scarphs, and in each case the one piece would slide sweetly and exactly into the other at the first trial. Then John would pass his hand gently over his work and smile a little at it, and I think, if the truth be known, that this was a species of caress bestowed by an artist upon a completed piece of work which appeared to him to be good. "She'll hold," Old John would say. "She'll hold; bolts or no bolts. Wet that and let her swell and she'll hold—for good an' all."

Two days of this kind of work sufficed to transform a pile of unrelated timbers into a species of girder which, for all intents and purposes, was stronger than if it had been cut out of one piece of wood. This girder was the foundation on which the rest of the schooner's hull would be built. It was the *Southseaman*'s keel in the rough, and at that stage it looked something like this:—

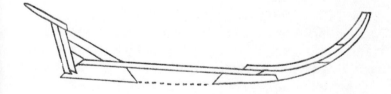

I say it looked "something" like that, because, as usual, I have managed to get the whole affair considerably out of drawing; and also the picture is made from memory only, and my memory for details is atrocious. However, the thing will serve to illustrate how the various scarphs were reinforced, and you will note that the boat's backbone was a very strong one. And it must be remembered that the floor timbers are yet to be laid athwart the keel, with the keelson and its members running along the top of them, and that the whole business is then fastened together with bolts which reach from the top of the keelson, right through everything, to the bottom of the keel. When this was done, and the frames and deck beams put in, you could, as Tom said, have rolled the boat down a cliff and not hurt her much.

George was a very busy man during those first delightful days in which, at last, the form of our boat began to take shape. He sent letters all over the continent of America, it seemed to me, concerning steering gears and tracks and water-closets and all those other things it was our business to secure. And after his letters he despatched telegrams, and once he even dashed off to Halifax to argue with the people who were busy casting our keel. At least I supposed them to be thus employed; but George thought otherwise, and he judged it advisable to go and urge them personally to their best endeavours. The speed with which the Sheldon craftsmen were carrying out their part of the work rather frightened George, I think, for he said, as he departed, "I'm going to get that keel here by the time they're ready for it, J., if I have to bring it down under my arm." And then George climbed into his buggy and dashed off. And I looked at the spidery wheels of that vehicle and became a little troubled, for there was over four tons of keel to come—plus a ton of George. But I did not remain troubled long, for I knew George for a man of resource (he *was,* as you shall see), so while he worried and worked, I remained perfectly idle and enjoyed myself.

Most of the time I would sit in the sun watching my schooner grow. I did no work at all, and, better still, I had good, comfortable, satisfactory reasons for continuing in this condition of peaceful sloth; for one day, when Old John was cutting out the rabbit on the keel, I had been misguided enough to ask him if I could be of help. And Old John had gazed at me for a little while before he replied. Then, "I guess not, Mister," said he, grinning, "for 'tis all brain work here today." That let me out, so I retired, much relieved, and sat me down on a stack of aromatic pine-boards, and warmed my back in the sun. I wonder if, in this life, there is any sensation more perfect than being free to look on, with your body at ease and your mind at peace, while men who are artists at their craft are fashioning at last, before your very eyes, the ship that has been for years, and years and years and years—merely a dream?

I wonder.

There was not a great deal of the perfect ship for me to look at during the first days, while the framework of her keel lay on its side in the shed with the floors and frames stacked in piles beside it. A stranger might have glanced into the shed then and not known that a ship was being built there. The groundways and the blocks were there, of course, but there was no shadow of a ship upon them. The time of preparation lasted, perhaps, a week, and then—suddenly—in a few hours— there was the *Southseaman* standing in the stocks. Her well-clothed skeleton materialised there at least; and to me, watching with bulging eyes, this emergence seemed rather like magic. It was very simple really, I suppose, for the timbers were all prepared and ready for assembling. But it is rather surprising, if you are not used to it, to see a set of vacant empty ways at 8 o'clock in the morning, and at 4 p.m. to find them occupied by a ship that looks as if she were already half completed. For a ship, in frame, looks a great deal more advanced than she really is; and when her keel is laid, with the stem and sternpost already in position, and her floors and frames are clamped into their places and held there by temporary shores and battens, she forthwith ceases to be merely an odd collection of timbers, and becomes— a ship. When you look at her then you can see, for the very first time, her *form;* and it is from that moment, and not until then, that she really begins to impress her various characteristics upon you.

You will understand, therefore, that it was a great moment for me when I found myself actually walking round and round my boat, *touching* her and *seeing* her at last. That morning there was nothing there at all, and, in the evening, there I was climbing all over the perfect ship.

It was a great moment.

I stood off at last and gazed at my boat from all possible angles until I was sure she was all I had meant her to be. I was very happy; and I was running my eye along the fine lines of her entrance when Tom came up and unwittingly disturbed my great content of mind. "Looks fine," said he.

I started, for at that moment those rather hollow water-lines were holding my critical eye. "What do you mean by that exactly, Tom?" said I. Tom, I think, was a little surprised at my tone, but "I said she looks all right. She looks fine, I think; don't you?" he answered.

"To tell you the truth, I do, Tom," I said. "And that's just what's beginning to trouble me." And at that I walked away, leaving Tom, I fear, a little mystified. I walked away until I reached the pile of iron pigs that were destined to form the schooner's inside ballast. I counted them, and there were sixty of them; and then I lifted one. Under certain circumstances 50lb. can seem very light. "I've a darned good mind," I said to myself, "to order another ton of them—in case!"

4   *A Great Ship Dies*

COMDR. LIGHTOLLER

I T had now become apparent that the ship was doomed, and in consequence I began to load the boats to the utmost capacity that I dared. My scheme for filling up at the lower deck doors had gone by the board—they were under water.

Many were the instances of calm courage.

One young couple walked steadily up and down the boat deck throughout pretty well the whole of the proceedings. Once or twice the young chap asked if he could help. He was a tall, clean-bred Britisher, on his honeymoon I should say. The girl—she was little more —never made the slightest attempt to come towards the boats, much less to be taken on board, although I looked towards her several times with a sort of silent invita-

77

tion, but no, she was not going to be parted from her man.

The order implicitly obeyed was, "Women and children only." The very highest tribute that it was possible for a human being to pay would hardly do justice to or give the praise due to the sheer calm courage shown by men, women and children amongst the passengers on that ship, individually and collectively. It made me unutterably proud of the English speaking race. The conditions were all strange; the ship was sinking and the boats were leaving, yet, neither man nor woman attempted to get into a boat without being ordered.

In the case of a Major Peuchen, a Canadian by birth, who went away in one of the boats, unwarrantable blame was attached, at a later date.

I was reduced to sending one seaman away in a boat, and on an occasion, after ordering away a sailor to take charge, I turned round to find there was only one left to attend the boat falls, for lowering away.

"Someone for that after fall," I called, and the next thing a man who had sailed with me for many years, Hemming by name, replied, "Aye, aye, sir! all ready." Unknown to me he had stepped out of the boat, back on board, to carry out what he considered the more important duty. Bravery and self-sacrifice such as this was of common occurrence throughout the night.

The boat was half way down when someone hailed me, saying, "We've no seamen in the boat," and at that moment I had no one available. I called to the people standing around, "Any seaman there?" No reply, and it was then that Major Peuchen, when he saw that there were none of the ship's crew available, said, "I'm not a seaman, but I'm a yachtsman, if I can be of any use to you."

The boat's falls, or ropes, by which the boat is lowered, hang up and down from the davit head, about nine or ten feet away from the ship's side. I said to him, "If you're seaman enough to get out on those falls, and get down into the boat you may go ahead." He did, and has been very unfairly criticised for carrying out what was a direct order.

* * *

As I returned along the deck, I passed Mr. and Mrs. Strauss leaning up against the deck house, chatting quite cheerily. I stopped and asked Mrs. Strauss, "Can I take you along to the boats?" She replied, "I think I'll stay here for the present." Mr. Strauss, calling her by her Christian name, said smilingly, "Why don't you go along with him, dear?" She just smiled, and said, "No, not yet." I left them, and they went down together. To another couple, evidently from the Western States, that I found sitting on a fan casing I asked the girl, "Won't you let me put you in one of the boats?" She replied with a very frank smile, "Not on your life. We started together, and if need be we'll finish together." It was typical of the spirit throughout.

Boat after boat was safely lowered into the water, with its human freight of women and children, each with an ever-increasing cargo as it became more and more evident that the *Titanic* was doomed, and that the ship to which we had looked for immediate help, was also a false hope. Time and again I had used her lights as a means to buoy up the hopes of the many that I now knew only too well, were soon to find themselves struggling in that icy water.

Why *couldn't* she hear our wireless calls? Why *couldn't* her Officer of the Watch or some one of her crew, see our distress signals with their showers of stars, visible for miles and miles around?—a signal that is never used except when a ship is in dire need of assistance. What wouldn't I have given for a six inch gun and a couple of shells to wake them up. I had assured and reassured the passengers throughout these anxious hours, "She cannot help but see these signals, and must soon steam over and pick everyone up." And what an absolutely unique opportunity Captain Lord, of the *Californian,* had that night of rendering aid and saving close on 1,500 lives. Nothing could have been easier than to have laid his ship actually alongside the *Titanic* and taken every soul on board. Yet, not a thing was done, not even was their wireless operator aroused to see if there *were* any distress calls.

There are no police, fire brigades or lifeboats out at sea, therefore it becomes nothing less than a fetish—the tenet above all tenets in the religion among sailors, that absolutely no effort shall be spared in an endeavour to save life at sea. A man must even be prepared to hazard his ship and his life.

Just before launching the last two lifeboats, I had made my final hurried visit to the stairway. It was then conclusively evident that not only *was* she going, but that she was going *very soon,* and if we were to avoid the unutterable disgrace of going down with lifeboats still hanging to the davits, there was not one single moment to lose.

Hurrying back to the two remaining lifeboats still hanging in their davits, I met the Purser, Assistant Purser, and the Senior and Junior Surgeons—the latter, a noted wag, even in the face of tragedy, couldn't resist his last mild joke, "Hello, Lights, are you warm?" The idea of anyone being warm in that temperature was a joke in itself, and I suppose it struck him as odd to meet me wearing a sweater, no coat or overcoat. I had long since discarded my greatcoat, even in pants and sweater over pyjamas alone I was in a bath of perspiration. There was only time to pass a few words, then they all shook hands and said "Good-bye." Frankly, I didn't feel at all like "Good-bye," although I knew we shouldn't have the ship under us much longer. The thing was to get these boats away at all costs. Eventually, and to my great relief, they were all loaded and safely lowered into the water.

The last lifeboat having got away, there remained No. 2 boat, which was actually a small sea boat used for emergency purposes (in fact often termed "The Emergency Boat"), hanging in the davits.

About this time I met all the engineers, as they came trooping up from below. Most of them I knew individually, and had been shipmates with them on different ships of the Line. They had all loyally stuck to their guns, long after they could be of any material assistance. Much earlier on the engine-room telegraphs had been "Rung off—" the last ring made on board ships at sea, and which conveys to the engine-room staff the final information that their services below can be of no further use, that the case (from whatever cause) is hopeless. At the same time it releases engineers and stokers from duty, leaving them free to make the best of their way to the boats. Of course, in theory, each has his appointed place in a given boat.

Since the *Titanic* disaster, each undoubtedly has. But before that tragedy brought home to the world the utter fallacy of the "unsinkable ship" I'm afraid that many "appointed places"—as far as life-saving equipment was concerned—were just so much theory, concocted ashore with a keen eye to dividends.

Certainly there was no sailor who ever sailed salt water but who smiled—and still smiles—at the idea of the "unsinkable ship".

There was little opportunity to say more than a word or two to the engineers. Up to that time they had known little of what was going on, and it was surely a bleak and hopeless spectacle that met their eyes. Empty falls

F

hanging loosely from every davit head, and not a solitary hope for any one of them.

In point of fact, they were lost to a man, *not one single survivor* out of the whole thirty-five.

* * *

"Any more women and children?" was the cry, and we had the greatest difficulty in finding sufficient to fill even this small boat—of those who were willing to go and leave others behind. Eventually, she was filled, and we lowered her away.

There now only remained two folded boats of the Engleheart type, with collapsible canvas sides, one on the deck by the davits of No. 2 emergency and one on top of the officers' quarters, both firmly lashed down. The rope falls of No. 2 were hurriedly rounded up and one collapsible boat hooked on and swung out ready for lowering.

I stood partly in the boat, owing to the difficulty of getting the womenfolk over a high bulwark rail just here. As we were ready for lowering the Chief came over to my side of the deck and, seeing me in the boat and no seaman available said, "You go with her, Lightoller."

Praises be, I had just sufficient sense to say, "Not damn likely," and jump back on board; not with any idea of self-imposed martyrdom—far from it—it was just pure impulse of the moment, and an impulse for which I was to thank my lucky stars a thousand times over, in the days to come. I had taken my chance and gone down with the rest, consequently I didn't have to take any old back-chat from anyone.

As this boat was being lowered, two men passengers jumped into her from the deck below. This, as far as I know, was the only instance of men getting away in boats from the port side. I don't blame them, the boat wasn't full, for the simple reason we couldn't find sufficient women, and there was no time to wait—the water was then actually lapping round their feet on "A" deck, so they jumped for it and got away. Good luck to them.

With one other seaman I started to cast adrift the one remaining Engleheart on top of the officer's quarters. We cut and threw off the lashings, jumped round to the inboard side ready to pick up the gunwale together and throw her bodily down on to the boat deck. The seaman working with me called:

"All ready, sir," and I recognised Hemming's voice— the chap I had ordered away long before, and who returned on board to tend the falls, and in whose place I sent Major Peuchen.

"Hello, is that you, Hemming?"

"Yes, sir."

"Why haven't you gone?" I asked.

"Oh, plenty of time yet, sir," he replied cheerily. Apparently the chap had loyally stuck by me all through, though it had been too dark to recognise him. Stout fellow. Later, he slid down one of the falls, swam for it and was saved.

We had just time to tip the boat over, and let her drop into the water that was now above the boat deck, in the hope that some few would be able to scramble on to her as she floated off. Hemming and I then, as every single boat was now away from the port side, went over to the starboard side, to see if there was anything further to be done there. But all the boats on this side had also been got away, though there were still crowds of people on the deck.

Just then the ship took a slight but definite plunge probably a bulkhead went—and the sea came rolling up in a wave, over the steel-fronted bridge, along the deck below us, washing the people back in a dreadful huddled mass. Those that didn't disappear under the water right away, instinctively started to clamber up that part of the deck still out of water, and work their way towards the stern, which was rising steadily out of the water as the bow went down. A few of the more agile leapt up on top of the officers' quarters where Hemming and I were at the moment. It was a sight that doesn't bear dwelling on—to stand there, above the wheelhouse, and on our quarters, watching the frantic struggles to climb up the sloping deck, utterly unable to even hold out a helping hand.

I knew, only too well, the utter futility of following that driving instinct of self-preservation and struggling up towards the stern. It would only be postponing the plunge, and prolonging the agony—even lessening one's already slim chances, by becoming one of a crowd. It came home to me very clearly how fatal it would be to get amongst those hundreds and hundreds of people who would shortly be struggling for their lives in that deadly cold water. There was only one thing to do, and I might just as well do it and get it over, so, turning to the fore part of the bridge, I took a header. Striking the water, was like a thousand knives being driven into one's body, and, for a few moments, I completely lost grip of myself—and no wonder for I was perspiring freely, whilst the temperature of the water was 28° (F), or 4° below freezing.

Ahead of me the look-out cage on the foremast was visible just above the water—in normal times it would be a hundred feet above. I struck out blindly for this, but only for a short while, till I got hold of myself again and realised the futility of seeking safety on anything connected with the ship. I then turned to starboard, away from the ship altogether.

The water was now pouring down the stokeholds, by way of the fiddley gratings abaft the bridge, and round the forward funnel.

On the boat deck, above our quarters, on the fore

part of the forward funnel, was a huge rectangular air shaft and ventilator, with an opening about twenty by fifteen feet. On this opening was a light wire grating to prevent rubbish being drawn down or anything else being thrown down. This shaft led direct to No. 3 stokehold, and was therefore a sheer drop of close on a hundred feet, right to the bottom of the ship.

I suddenly found myself drawn, by the sudden rush of the surface water now pouring down this shaft, and held flat and firmly up against this wire netting with the additional full and clear knowledge of what would happen if this light wire carried away. The pressure of the water just glued me there whilst the ship sank slowly below the surface.

Although I struggled and kicked for all I was worth, it was impossible to get away, for as fast as I pushed myself off I was irresistibly dragged back, every instant expecting the wire to go, and to find myself shot down into the bowels of the ship.

Apart from that, I was drowning, and a matter of another couple of minutes would have sent me through. I was still struggling and fighting when suddenly a terrific blast of hot air came up the shaft, and blew me right away from the air shaft and up to the surface.

The water was now swirling round, and the ship sinking rapidly, when once again I was caught and sucked down by an inrush of water, this time adhering to one of the fiddley gratings. Just how I got clear of that, I don't know, as I was rather losing interest in things, but I eventually came to the surface once again, this time alongside that last Engleheart boat which Hemming and I had launched from on top of the officers' quarters on the opposite side—for I was now on the starboard side, near the forward funnel.

There were many around in the water by this time, some swimming, others (mostly men, thank God), definitely drowning—an utter nightmare of both sight and sound. In the circumstances I made no effort to get on top of the upturned boat, but, for some reason, was content to remain floating alongside, just hanging on to a small piece of rope.

The bow of the ship was now rapidly going down and the stern rising higher and higher out of the water, piling the people into helpless heaps around the steep decks, and by the score into the icy water. Had the boats been around many might have been saved, but of them, at this time there was no sign. Organised help, or even individual help, was quite impossible. All one could do was just wait on events, and try and forget the icy grip of the water.

When I again recognised my surroundings, we were fully fifty yards clear of the ship. The piece of rope was still in my hand, with old friend Engleheart upturned and attached to the other end, with several men by now standing on it. I also scrambled up, after spending longer than I like to remember in that icy water. Lights on board the *Titanic* were still burning, and a wonderful spectacle she made, standing out black and massive against the starlit sky; myriads of lights still gleaming through the portholes, from that part of the decks still above water.

The fore part and up to the second funnel was by this time completely submerged, and as we watched this terribly awe-inspiring sight, suddenly all lights went out and the huge bulk was left in black darkness, but clearly silhouetted against the bright sky. Then, the next moment, the massive boilers left their beds and went thundering down with a hollow rumbling roar, through the bulk-heads, carrying everything with them that stood in their way. This unparalleled tragedy that was being enacted before our very eyes, now rapidly approached its finale, as the huge ship slowly but surely reared herself on end and brought rudder and propellers clear of the water, till, at last, she assumed *an absolute perpendicular position*. In this amazing attitude she remained for the space of half a minute. Then with impressive majesty and ever increasing momentum, she silently took her last tragic dive to seek a final resting place in the unfathomable depths of the cold grey Atlantic.

5 *The Character of the Foe*

JOSEPH CONRAD

IT seems to me that no man born and truthful to himself could declare that he ever saw the sea looking young as the earth looks young in spring. But some of us, regarding the ocean with understanding and affection, have seen it looking old, as if the immemorial ages had been stirred up from the undisturbed bottom of ooze. For it is a gale of wind that makes the sea look old.

From a distance of years, looking at the remembered aspects of the storms lived through, it is that impression which disengages itself clearly from the great body of impressions left by many years of intimate contact.

If you would know the age of the earth, look upon the sea in a storm. The greyness of the whole immense surface, the wind furrows upon the faces of the waves, the great masses of foam, tossed about and waving, like matted white locks, give to the sea in a gale an appearance of hoary age, lustreless, dull, without gleams, as though it had been created before light itself.

Looking back after much love and much trouble, the instinct of primitive man, who seeks to personify the forces of Nature for his affection and for his fear, is awakened again in the breast of one civilized beyond that stage even in his infancy. One seems to have known gales as enemies, and even as enemies one embraces them in that affectionate regret which clings to the past.

Gales have their personalities, and, after all, perhaps it is not strange; for, when all is said and done, they are adversaries whose wiles you must defeat, whose violence you must resist, and yet with whom you must live in the intimacies of nights and days.

Here speaks the man of the masts and sails, to whom the sea is not a navigable element, but an intimate companion. The length of passages, the growing sense of solitude, the close dependence upon the very forces that, friendly today, without changing their nature, by the mere putting forth of their might, become dangerous tomorrow, make for that sense of fellowship which modern seamen, good men as they are, cannot hope to know. And, besides, your modern ship which is a steamship makes her passages on other principles than yielding to the weather and humouring the sea. She receives smashing blows, but she advances; it is a slogging fight, and not a scientific campaign. The machinery, the steel, the fire, the steam have stepped in between the man and the sea. A modern fleet of ships does not so much make use of the sea as exploit a highway. The modern ship is not the sport of the waves. Let us say that each of her voyages is a triumphant progress; and yet it is a question whether it is not a more subtle and more human triumph to be the sport of the waves and yet survive, achieving your end.

In his own time a man is always very modern. Whether the seamen of three hundred years hence will have the faculty of sympathy it is impossible to say. An incorrigible mankind hardens its heart in the progress of its own perfectability. How will they feel on seeing the illustrations to the sea novels of our day, or of our yesterday? It is impossible to guess. But the seaman of the last generation, brought into sympathy with the caravels of ancient time by his sailing-ship, their lineal descendant, cannot look upon those lumbering forms navigating the naïve seas of ancient woodcuts without a feeling of surprise, of affectionate derision, envy, and admiration. For those things, whose unmanageableness, even when represented on paper makes one gasp with a sort of amused horror, were manned by men who are his direct professional ancestors.

No; the seamen of three hundred years hence will probably be neither touched nor moved to derision, affection, or admiration. They will glance at the photo-gravures of our nearly defunct sailing-ships with a cold, inquisitive, and indifferent eye. Our ships of yesterday will stand to their ships as no lineal ancestors, but as mere predecessors whose course will have been run and the race extinct. Whatever craft he handles with skill, the seaman of the future shall be not our descendant, but only our successor.

6 *Gipsy Moth Circles the World*

ALAN VILLIERS

IFIRST met Sir Francis Chichester—plain Francis then—when he was a pioneer airman trying to get backing for an early flight from London to Sydney. He was an earnest young man with a strong face and very thick glasses. I wondered how he'd managed to qualify for a pilot's licence. He already had the airplane, a little De Havilland Moth biplane with a Gipsy engine. Almost unique among pioneer airmen, he'd bought that himself. He wished only to sell the story. There were no buyers. He flew anyway, and made it. It took a long time—six months, I seem to remember. It was a colossal exhibition of guts, endurance, and flying skill. After that, in between long intervals, I heard of him—trying to fly another minute biplane round the world, bashing into some overhead cables (which he hadn't seen) over a harbour in Japan. He was dragged out of the wreckage, said the news flash, and given ten minutes to live. Ten minutes? That was nearly 40 years ago. Next, he was flying a single-engined float-plane, another Gipsy Moth, across the Tasman Sea, a nasty piece of water that links the Coral Sea to the Antarctic between New Zealand and Australia. To make it, he had to pick up a couple of pinpoint islands hundreds of miles apart and far from anywhere, without landing facilities or navigational aids apart from a lighthouse each for surface ships. He made them both, bashed a float off in a bumpy landing at Lord Howe, put the float back on and flew to Sydney. I noted Francis Chichester as a fellow who did what he set out to do, regardless, though he was apt to knock himself about a bit in the process and put heavy strains on small aircraft. He could write, too.

Nobody paid much attention. He wasn't at all the flamboyant type. He was a loner who financed himself and got on with whatever it was he'd undertaken, come what may.

I was surprised at first when I heard he'd taken up yacht-racing, some years after the war. When I learned that it was single-handed racing across the North Atlantic he'd taken on, I understood. Here was something else where he could cope with all the challenges himself, drive himself and bother nobody, do the job his way, succeed—or else. The success if any would be his, and the calamities likewise. Whatever else Francis Chichester was and is, he is no joiner. "Blondie" Hasler, former Marine cockleshell hero, organised the first single-handed yacht race westwards over the North Atlantic in 1960: Francis Chichester won it. He won the second, too (against himself, failing other entries), and came a very creditable second in the third.

What next? The man was past 60. A serious illness had been diagnosed as lung cancer. He had a good business map-publishing in London. Anybody else might have sat back. So he dreamt up the idea of a single-handed sail right around the world—and not for him the simpler way, westwards with the N.E. Trades, through Panama Canal, westwards again with the Trades of the South Seas, a romp across the Indian and home around Good Hope. No, he planned to go the old square-rigger way, the *tough* way, out round Good Hope then "run his Easting down" and in high latitudes to Australia; homeward thence in even higher latitudes, taking on the Horn. As if that weren't enough, he was going to race on the way, too—not with any other yacht (none offered) but against what he'd worked out to be average "clipper" times of last century.

Very largely, he specified the kind of yacht for the job—the biggest, fastest ketch one man might handle, with the most diversified suit of sails. He hadn't been able to design his own airplanes, having to content himself in that field with inventing some remarkable navigation methods and devices. A globe-circling "clipper" yacht was a different thing. John Illingworth did the drawings for the sort of thing Chichester thought he wanted, Charles Blake built it at Gosport. It turned out to be a 53ft. ketch, tender, high-strung, not at all suitable I thought for a single-handed job anywhere and a "killer" down south in the Roaring Forty gales. I showed him some film I'd made running for the Horn in the ship *Joseph Conrad,* with the full-rigger tossed about in the nasty great seas forever raging at her and all but over her. It shook him; but it made no difference. Off he went, alone . . . out of the Channel, through the "Horse latitudes" and southward with the N.E. Trades, across

the Line in the dribbling Doldrums, through the S.E.
Trades, and then into the grim turmoil of the South
Indian Ocean's westerly gales, one after the other,
screaming at him, making a toy of his course-keeping
device (sturdy as it was) while the seas flung his ketch
about in an endless effort to wear him out, destroy him
body and mind. He came into Sydney 109 days out—
good for a big windjammer but no clipper run—more
dead than alive, disappointed with his yacht which had
not come up to his hopes and proved a bit of a wet
tough nut to handle.

He'd done enough. It was a splendid feat already.
Why take on the Horn? There were quieter ways back—
up through the Coral Sea for one, inside the Barrier
Reef (the way Conrad had taken the barque *Otago*
once, bound for Mauritius). The knowledgeable shook
their heads about that yacht and about its master, who
had taken a great deal out of himself. Had he more to
give? He was a sick man. It never occurred to him not
to continue as planned. The Australian designers,
familiar with the Tasman Sea, made what useful altera-
tions to the Gipsy Moth IV they could—lengthening the
keel, improving the course-keeping device and a lead or
two in the gear here and there. Towards the end of
January with a Coral Sea cyclone warning for the
northern Tasman Sea, Chichester took his big ketch to
sea again—alone, determined, still fascinated by that
"clipper" way. Within a week the contemptuous seas
had flung him on his beam-ends, stove his fore-hatch in,
come near to sinking his Gipsy Moth before he was out
of the Tasman Sea. She righted herself; he baled her
out. One concession he made, then: he eased her off to
run around the northern end of New Zealand, and kept
her more to the nor'ard than he'd meant to do, on much
of the long run towards the Horn. The gales found him
there, of course. Again the yacht pitched and stumbled

and hurtled on, never for an instant still, never for a second dry on deck. She did her best to throw him overboard but he lashed himself and carried on.

He was 55 days from Sydney to the Horn (the real clippers tried to make it in from 20 to 30). But he made it; and was disgusted to see a British warship patrolling there to see him round (or get pictures for the world press) and more so when a light aircraft buzzed him, full of reporters. Well, he was past the Horn, and staggered contentedly about the reeling deck setting a little more sail to drive the yacht on for England.

Just over nine weeks later, 119 days out from Sydney, he came sailing into Plymouth Sound where the Hoe was black with cheering citizens by the hundred thousand. He had made no clipper passages but he had done what he set out to do. At the age of 65, sick, crusty, bashed about, he had forced himself to sail a really unsuitable vessel the best part of 29,000 miles, much of it across the stormiest seas in the world. He didn't have to be there. No yacht has to make such passages and gains nothing perhaps by attempting them. But it was a remarkable feat of *guts,* a moving story of conquest by the unquenchable human spirit.

7   *The Promotion of the Admiral*

MORLEY ROBERTS

MR. SMITH, who ran a sailors' boarding-house
in that part of San Francisco known as the
Barbary Coast, was absolutely *sui generis*. If
any drunken scallawag of a scholar, who had drifted
ashore on his boarding-house mud-flats, had ventured
in a moment of alcoholic reminiscence to say so in the
classic tongue, Shanghai Smith would have "laid him
out cold" with anything handy, from a stone-ware
match-box to an empty bottle. But if that same son of
culture had used his mother tongue, as altered for popu-
lar use in the West, and had murmured: "Jerusalem
but Mr. Smith's the daisy of all!" Smith would have
thrown out his chest and blown through his teeth a
windy oath and guessed he was just so.

G

"Say it and mean it, that's me," said Smith. "I'm all right. But call me hog and I *am* hog; don't you forget it!"

Apparently all the world called him "hog." For that he was no better than one, whether he walked, or ate, or drank, or slept, was obvious to any sailor with an open eye. But he was hard and rough and tough, and had the bull-headed courage of a mad steer combined with the wicked cunning of a monkey.

So far as ships and sailormen were concerned he certainly spoke the truth. He was talked of with curses in the Pacific from the Prybiloffs to the Horn, from San Francisco to Zanzibar. It was long odds at any given time in any longitude that some seaman was engaged in blaspheming Shanghai Smith for sending him on board drunk and without a chest, and with nothing better to propitiate his new shipmates with than a bottle of vinegar and water that looked like rum till it was tasted. Every breeze that blew, trade wind or monsoon, had heard of his iniquities. He got the best of every one.

"All but one," said Smith in a moment of weakness, when a dozen men, who owed so much money that they crawled to him as a Chinaman does to a joss, were hanging upon his lips—"all but one."

"Oh, we don't take that in," said one of the most indebted; "we can 'ardly believe that, Mr. Smith."

He looked them over malignantly.

"I kin lick any of you here with one hand," he swore, "but the man as bested me could have taken on three of you with both hands. And I own I was took aback considerable when I run against him on the pier at Sandridge when I was in Australia fifteen years ago. He was a naval officer, captain of the *Warrior*, and dressed up to kill, though he had a face like a figure-head cut out of mahog'ny with a broad-axe. And I was feelin' good and in need of a scrap. So when he bumped agin me, I shoved him over—prompt, I shoved him. Down he went, and the girls that know'd me laughed. And two policemen came along quick. I didn't care much, but this naval josser picks himself up and goes to 'em. Would you believe it, but when he'd spoke a bit I seed him donate them about a dollar each and they walked off round a heap of dunnage on the wharf, and the captain buttoned up his coat and came for me. He comes up dancin' and smilin', and he kind of give me half a bow, polite as you like, and inside of ten seconds I knew I'd struck a cyclone, right in the spot where they breed. I fought good—(you know me)—and I got in half a dozen on his face. But I never fazed him none, and he wouldn't bruise mor'n hittin' a boiler. And every time he got back on me I felt as if I'd been kicked. He scarred me something cruel. I could see it by the blood on his hands. Twarn't his, by a long sight, for his fists was made of teak, I should say. When I came to, which was next day in a kind of sailors' hospital, I reached up for a card over my head, and I read 'concussion of the brain' on it. What's more, I believed it. If the card had let on that I'd been run over by a traction engine and picked up dead, I'd have believed it. And when I reely came to my senses, a med'cal student says as Captain Richard Dunn, of the *Warrior,* had bin to inquire when the funeral was, so's he could send a wreath. They said he was the topside fighter in the hull British Navy. And I'm here to say he was."

He breathed fierce defiance and invited any man alive to tell him he was lying.

"And you never got even?" asked the bar-tender, seeing that no one took up the challenge.

"Never set eyes on him from that day to this," said his boss regretfully.

"And if you did?"

Smith paused, took a drink.

"So help me, I'd Shanghai him if he was King of England!"

And one of the crowd, who had put down the *San Francisco Chronicle* in order to hear this yarn, picked it up again.

"S'elp me," he said, in a breathless excitement, " 'ere's a bally cohincidence. 'Ere's a telegram from 'Squimault, saying as how the flagship *Triumphant,* Hadmiral Sir Richard Dunn, K.C.B., is comin' down to San Francisco!"

"Holy Moses, let's look!" said Shanghai Smith.

He read, and a heavenly smile overspread his hard countenance.

"Tom," he said to the bar-tender, "set up the drinks for the crowd. This is my man, for sure. And him an admiral, too! Holy sailor, ain't this luck?"

The morning of the following day H.M.S. *Triumphant* lay at her anchors off Sausalito in San Francisco Bay, and was glad to be there. For this was in the times when the whole British fleet was not absolutely according to Cocker. She leaked not a little and she rolled a great deal, and she would not mind her helm except upon those occasions when the officer in charge of the deck laid his money and his reputation on her going to starboard when, according to all rules, she should have altered her course to port. But though she was a wet ship with a playful habit of trying to scoop the Pacific Ocean dry, and though her tricks would have broken the heart of the Chief Naval Constructor had he seen her at them, she was the flagship in spite of her conduct, because at that time she was half the whole Pacific Squadron. The other half was lying outside Esquimault Dry Dock waiting for it to be finished. And when the *Chronicle* said that "Dicky Dunn" was the admiral, it had not lied. If any of that paper's reporters had known "Dicky" as his men knew him, he would have spread himself in a column on the admiral's character and personal appearance.

Though he stood five feet nine in height, he looked two inches less, for he was as broad as a door and as sturdy as the fore-bitts. His complexion was the colour of the sun when it sets in a fog for fine weather: the skin on his hands shone and was as scaly as a lizard's hide. His teeth were white and his eyes piercing. He could roar like a fog-horn, and sing, as the crew said, "like any hangel". There wasn't the match of "Dicky" on any of the seas the wide world over. The only trouble was that he looked so much like the traditional sailor and buccaneer that no one could believe he was anything higher than a warrant officer at the most when he had none of his official gear about him.

Though the admiral did not know it, one of the very first to greet him when he set his foot on dry land at the bottom of Market Street was the man he had licked so thoroughly fifteen years before in Melbourne.

"Oh, it's the same," said Smith to his chief runner, who was about the "hardest case" in California. "He ain't changed none. Just so old he was when he set about me. Why, the galoot might be immortal. Mark him, now; will you know him anywhere?"

"It don't pay me ever to forget," replied the runner. He had to remember the men who owed him grudges.

"Then don't forget this one," said Smith. "Do you find me a considerate boss?"

"Oh well—" said the runner ungraciously.

"You've got to do a job for me, Bill."

"And what?"

"I'm goin' to have this hyer admiral shipped before the stick on the toughest ship that's about ready to go to sea," replied Smith.

Bill flinched.

"Sir, it's the penitentiary!"

"I don't care if it's lynchin'," said Smith. "Help—or get. I'm bossin' this job. Which is it?"

And Bill, seeing that he was to play second fiddle, concluded to help.

"Which do you reckon is the worst ship inside the Gate now?" asked Smith, after he had savoured his cunning revenge for a few minutes.

"There's the *Cyrus G. Hake*."

Smith shook his head contemptuously.

"D'ye think I want to board this admiral at the Palace Hotel? Why, Johnson hasn't hurt a man serious for two trips."

"Oh, well, I thought as he'd sure break out soon," said Bill; "but there's the *President*. They do say that her new mate is a holy terror."

"I won't go on hearsay," said Smith decidedly. "I want a good man you and I know—one that'll handle this Dicky Dunn from the start. Now, what's in the harbour with officers that can lick *me*?"

"Well, I always allowed (as you know, Mr. Smith) that Simpson of the *California* was your match."

Smith's face softened.

"Well, mebbe he is."

At any other time he would never have admitted it.

"And the *California* will sail in three days."

"Righto," said Smith. "Simpson is a good tough man and so is old Blaker. Bill, the *California* will do. But it's an almighty pity the *Harvester* ain't here.

"But how'll you corral the admiral, sir?" asked Bill.

"You leave that to me," replied his boss. "I've got a very fruitful notion as will fetch him if he's half the man he was."

Next evening Smith found occasion to run across a couple of the *Triumphant's* crew, and he got them to come into his house for a drink.

"Are these galoots to be dosed and put away?" asked the bar-tender.

"Certainly not," said Smith. "Fill 'em up with good honest liquor at my expense."

The bar-tender hardly knew where good honest liquor was to be found in that house, but he gave the two men-o'-war's men the slowest poison he had, and they were soon merry.

"Is the admiral as dead keen on fightin' with his fists as he was?" asked Smith.

"Rather," said the first man.

"Oh no, he's tired," said the second. " 'E allows 'e can't find no one to lick 'im. 'E never could."

"Oh, that's his complaint, is it?" asked Smith. "And is he as good as he was?"

"I heerd him tell the first luff' on'y the other day as 'e reckoned to be a better man now than he was twenty years ago. And I believes 'im. 'Ard? Oh my! I do believe if 'e ran agin a lamp-post he'd fight through it."

It was enough for Smith to know that the Admiral was still keen on fighting. To draw a man like that would not be so difficult. When he had turned the two naval seamen into the street, he called for the runner.

"Have you found out what I told you?"

"Yes," replied Bill. "He mostly comes down and goes off at eleven."

"Is he alone?"

"Mostly he has a young chap with him. I reckon they calls him the flag-lieutenant: a kind of young partner he seems to be. But that's the only one so far. And the *California* sails day after ter-morrer, bright and early."

"Couldn't be better," said Smith. "After waitin' all these years I can't afford to lose no time. This hyer racket comes off tonight. Look out, Mr. Bully Admiral! I'm on your track."

And the trouble did begin that night.

Mr. "Say-it-and-mean-it" Smith laid for Admiral Sir Richard Dunn, K.C.B., etc., etc., from ten o'clock till half-past eleven, and he was the only man in the crowd that did not hope that victim would come down with too many friends to be tackled.

"It's a penitentiary job, so it is," said Bill. And yet when the time arrived his natural instincts got the better of him.

The admiral came at last: it was about a quarter to twelve, and the whole water-front was remarkably quiet. The admiral was only accompanied by his flag-lieutenant.

"That's him," said Smith. "I'd know the beggar any-where. Now keep together and sing!"

He broke into "Down on the Suwannee River," and advanced with Bill and Bill's two mates right across the admiral's path. They pretended to be drunk, and as far as three were concerned, there was not so much pre-tence about it after all. But Smith had no intention of being the first to run athwart the admiral's hawse. When he came close enough, he shoved the youngest man right into his arms. The admiral jumped back, and landed that unfortunate individual a round-arm blow that nearly unshipped his jaw. The next moment every one was on the ground, for Bill sandbagged the admiral just as he was knocked down by the lieutenant. As Sir Richard fell, he reached out and caught Smith by the ankle. The boarding-house master got the lieutenant by the coat and brought him down too. And as luck would have it, the youngster's head hit the admiral's with such a crack that both lay unconscious.

"Do we want the young 'un too?" asked Bill when he rose to his feet, swinging his sand-bag savagely. And Smith for once lost his head.

"Leave the swine, and puckarow the admiral," he said. And indeed it was all they could do to carry Sir

Richard without exciting any more attention than four semi-intoxicated men would as they took home a mate who was quite incapacitated.

But they did get him home to the house in the Barbary Coast. When he showed signs of coming to, he was promptly dosed and his clothes were taken off him. As he slept the sleep of the drugged, they put on him a complete suit of rough serge toggery and he became "Tom Deane, A.B.".

"They do say that he is the roughest, toughest, hardest nut on earth," said Bill; "so we'll see what like he shapes in the *California*. I dessay he's one of that lot that let on how sailormen have an easy time. It's my notion the *California* will cure him of that."

By four o'clock in the morning, Tom Deane, who was, as his new shipmates allowed, a hard-looking man who could, and would, pull his weight, lay fast asleep in a forward bunk of the *California's* foc'sle as she was being towed through the Golden Gate. And his flag-lieutenant was inquiring in hospital what had become of the admiral, and nobody could tell him more than he himself knew. So much he told the reporters of the *Chronicle* and the *Morning Call,* and flaring headlines announced the disappearance of a British admiral, and the wires and cables fairly hummed to England and the world generally. At the same time the San Francisco police laid every waterfront rat and tough by the heels on the chance that something might be got out of one of them.

When the admiral woke, which he did after half an hour's shaking administered in turns by three of the *California's* crew, who were anxious to know where he had stowed his bottle of rum, he was still confused with the "dope" given him ashore. So he lay pretty still and said:

"Send Mr. Selwyn to me."

But Selwyn was his flag-lieutenant, and was just then the centre of interest to many reporters.

"Send hell; rouse out, old son, and turn to," said one of his new mates. And the admiral rose and rested on his elbow.

"Where am I?"

"On board the *California,* to be sure."

"I'm dreaming," said the admiral, "that's what it is. To be sure, I'm dreaming."

There was something in his accent as he made this statement that roused curiosity in the others.

"No, you ain't—not much," said the first man who had spoken; "and even if you was, I guess Simpson will wake you. Rouse up before he comes along again. He was in here an hour back inquiring for the trumpet of the Day of Judgment to rouse you. Come along, Deane! Now them!"

"My name's Dunn," said the admiral, with contracted brows.

"Devil doubt it," said his friend; "and who done you? Was it Shanghai Smith?"

The admiral sat up suddenly, and by so doing brought his head into violent contact with the deck above him. This woke him thoroughly, just in time to receive Mr. Simpson, mate of the *California,* who came in like a cyclone to inquire after his health.

"Did you ship as a dead man?" asked Mr. Simpson, "for if you did, I'll undeceive you."

And with that he yanked the admiral from his bunk, and dragged him by the collar out upon the deck at a run. Mr. Simpson was "bucko" to his finger-tips, and had never been licked upon the high seas. But for that matter Vice-Admiral Sir Richard Dunn, K.C.B., had never hauled down his flag either to any man. It surprised him, as it would have surprised any of his crew, to find that he took this handling almost meekly. But then no one knows what he would do if the sky fell; and as far as the admiral was concerned, the entire world was an absurd and ridiculous nightmare.

"Who—who are you?" he said.

Mr. Simpson gasped.

"Who am I—oh, who am I? Well, I'll oblige you by statin' once for all that I'm mate of this ship, and you're my dog."

But the "dog" shook his head.

"Nothing of the sort," he said, as he staggered with the remains of the opiate. "I'm a British admiral, and my name's Sir Richard Dunn. Where's my ship?"

"Oh, you're an admiral—an admiral, heh?" said Simpson.

"Of course," said Sir Richard, and a sudden gust of rage blew the last opium out of him. "Why, damn it, sir, what the devil do you mean by laying your filthy paws on me? Where's your captain, sir? By all that's holy, I'll smash you if you so much as look at me again."

Now it is a remarkable fact that the utterly and entirely unexpected will sometimes shake the courage of the stoutest heart. It is possible that a tiger would itself turn tail if a lamb rushed at him with open mouth. And though Mr. Simpson would have tackled a prize-fighter, knowing he was a prize-fighter, the fact that one of the kind of men whom he was accustomed to wipe his boots on now turned upon him with entirely strange language and a still stranger air of authority, for a moment daunted him utterly. He stood still and gasped, while the admiral strode aft and went up the poop ladder. He was met there by the captain, who had been the terror of the seas as a mate. A narrow escape of a conviction for murder had partially reformed him. He had also become religious, and usually went below when Simpson or the second "greaser" was hammering anyone into oblivion and obedience.

"What is this?" asked Captain Blaker mildly, yet with a savage eye. "Mr. Simpson, what do you mean by allowing your authority (and mine delegated to you) to be disregarded?"

"Sir—" said Mr. Simpson, and then the admiral turned on him.

"Hold your infernal tongue, sir," he roared. "And, sir, if you are the master of this vessel, as I suppose, I require you to put about for San Francisco. I am a British admiral, sir; my name is Sir Richard Dunn."

"Oh, you're an admiral and you 'require'?" said Blaker. "Wa'al, I do admire! You look like an admiral: the water-front is full of such. Take that, sir."

And the resurgent old Adam in Blaker struck the admiral with such unexpected force that Dunn went heels over head off the poop and landed on Simpson. The mate improved the opportunity by kicking him violently in the ribs. When he was tired, he spoke to the admiral again.

"Now, you lunatic, take this here ball of twine and go and overhaul the gear on the main. And if you open your mouth to say another word I'll murder you."

And though he could not believe he was doing it, Sir Richard Dunn crawled aloft, and did what he was told. He was stunned by his fall and the hammering he had received, but that was nothing to the utter and complete change of air that he experienced. As he overhauled the gear he wondered if he was an admiral at all. If he was, how came he on the maintopgallant-yard of a merchant ship? If he wasn't, why was he surprised at being there? He tried to recall the last day of his life as an admiral, and was dimly conscious of a late evening somewhere in San Francisco at which he had certainly taken his share of liquor.

"I—I must be mad," said the admiral.

"Now then, look alive there, you dead crawling cat," said Mr. Simpson, "or I'll come up and boot you off the yard. Do you hear me?"

"Yes, sir," said the admiral quickly, and as he put a new mousing on the clip-hooks of the mizzen-topmast-staysail-tripping-line block, he murmured: "I suppose I never was an admiral after all. I don't seem to know what I am."

"He's crazy," said Simpson to the second greaser. "Says he's an admiral. I've had the Apostle Peter on board, and a cook who said he was St. Paul, but this is the first time I've run against an admiral before the mast."

"Does he look like it, sir?" asked Wiggins, laughing.

"He looks the toughest case you ever set eyes on," said Simpson. "But you'd have smiled to see the way the old man slugged him off the poop. And yet there's something about him I don't tumble to. I guess that's where his madness lies. Guess I'll cure him or kill him by the time we get off Sandy Hook—Now then, you admiral, come down here and start up the fore rigging, and do it quick, or I'll know the reason why."

And the Knight Commander of the Bath came down as he was bid, and having cast a perplexed eye over Simpson and Wiggins, who sniggered at him with amused and savage contempt, he went forward in a hurry.

"This is a nightmare," he said; "I'm dreaming. Damme, perhaps I'm dead!"

When he had overhauled the gear at the fore—and being a real seaman, he did it well—Wiggins called him down to work on deck, and he found himself among his new mates. By now they were all aware that he believed he was an admiral, and that he had spoken to Simpson in a way that no man had ever done. That was so much to his credit, but since he was mad he was a fit object of jeers. They jeered him accordingly, and when they were at breakfast the trouble began.

"Say, are you an admiral?" asked Knight, the biggest tough on board except Simpson and Wiggins.

And the admiral did not answer. He looked at Knight with a gloomy, introspective eye.

"Mind your own business," he said, when the question was repeated.

And Knight hove a full pannikin of tea at him. This compliment was received very quietly, and the admiral rose and went on deck.

"Takes water at once," said Knight; "he ain't got the pluck of a mouse.'

But the admiral went aft and interviewed Mr. Simpson.

"May I have the honour of speaking to you, sir?" he said, and Simpson gasped a little, but said he might have that honour.

"Well, sir," said Sir Richard Dunn, "I don't know how I got here, but here I am, and I'm willing to waive the question of my being a British admiral, as I can't prove it."

"That's right," said Simpson.

The admiral nodded.

"But I wish to have your permission to knock the head off a man called Knight for'ard. It was always my custom, sir, to allow fights on board my own ship when I considered them necessary. But I always insisted on my permission being asked. Have I yours, sir?"

Simpson looked the admiral up and down.

"Your ship, eh? You're still crazy, I'm afraid. But Knight can kill you, my man."

"I'm willing to let him try, sir," said the admiral. "He hove a pannikin of tea over me just now, and I think a thrashing would do him good and conduce to the peace and order of the foc'sle."

"Oh, you think so," said Simpson. "Very well, you have my permission to introduce peace there."

"I thank you, sir," said the admiral.

He touched his hat and went forward. He put his head inside the foc'sle and addressed Knight:

"Come outside, you bully, and let me knock your head off. Mr. Simpson has been kind enough to overlook the breach of discipline involved."

And Knight, nothing loth, came out on deck, while Simpson and Wiggins stood a little way off to enjoy the battle.

"I'd like to back the admiral," said Wiggins.

"I'll have a level five dollars on Knight," said Simpson, who remembered that he had, on one occasion, found Knight extremely difficult to reduce to pulp.

"Done with you," said Wiggins.

And in five minutes the second mate was richer by five dollars, as his mates carried Knight into the foc'sle.

"I don't know when I enjoyed myself more," said Simpson, with a sigh—"even if I do lose money on it. While it lasted it was real good. Did you see that most be-ewtiful upper cut? And the right-handed cross counter that finished it was jest superb. But I'll hev to speak to the victor, so I will."

And he addressed the admiral in suitable language.

"Don't you think, because you've licked him, that you can fly any flag when I'm around. You done it neat and complete, and I overlook it, but half a look and the fust letter of a word of soss and I'll massacre you myself. Do you savvy?"

And the admiral said: "Yes, sir."

He touched his cap and went forward to the foc'sle to enter into his kingdom. For Knight had been "topside joss" there for three voyages, being the only man who had ever succeeded in getting even one pay-day out of the *California*. The principle on which she was run was to make things so hot for her crew that they skipped out at New York instead of returning to San Francisco, and the fresh crew shipped in New York did the same when they got inside the Golden Gate.

"I understand," said the admiral, as he stood in the middle of the foc'sle, "that the gentleman I've just had the pleasure of knocking into the middle of next week was the head bully here. Now I want it thoroughly understood in future that if any bullying is to be done, I'm going to do it."

All the once obedient slaves of the deposed Knight hastened to make their peace with the new power. They fairly crawled to the admiral.

"You kin fight," said one.

"I knew it jest so soon as you opened yer mouth," said another. "The tone of yer voice argued you could."

"It's my belief that he could knock the stuffin' out o' Mr. Simpson," said the third.

" 'Twould be the best kind of fun," said another admirer of the powers that be, "for Blaker would kick Simpson in here, and give the admiral his job right off. He's got religion, has Blaker, but he was an old packet rat himself, and real 'bucko' he was, and believes in the best men bein' aft."

And though the admiral said nothing to this, he remembered it, and took occasion to inquire into its truth. He found that what he knew of the sea and its customs was by no means perfect. He learnt something every day, and not least from Knight, who proved by no means a bad sort of man when he had once met his match.

"Is it true," asked the admiral, "what they say about Captain Blaker giving anyone the mate's job if he can thrash him?"

"It used to be the custom in the Western Ocean," said Knight, "and Blaker was brought up there. He's a real sport, for all his bein' sort of religious. Yes, I'll bet it's true." He turned to the admiral suddenly. "Say, you wasn't thinkin' of takin' Simpson on, was you?"

"If what you say's true, I was," said the admiral. "It don't suit me being here."

"Say now, partner," put in Knight, "what's this guff about your being an admiral? What put it into your head?"

And Sir Richard Dunn laughed. As he began to feel his feet, and find that he was as good a man in new surroundings as in the old ones, he recovered his courage and his command of himself.

"After all, this will be the deuce of a joke when it's over," he thought, "and I don't see why I shouldn't get a discharge out of her as mate. Talk about advertisement!"

He knew how much it meant.

"Look here, Knight," he said aloud, "I *am* an admiral. I can't prove it, but my ship was the *Triumphant*. I don't want to force it down your throat, but if you'd say you believe it, I should be obliged to you."

Knight put out his hand.

"I believes it, sonny," he said, "for I own freely that there's suthin' about you different from us; a way of talk, and a look in the eye that ain't formiliar in no foc'sle as I ever sailed in. No, I believe you're speakin' the trewth."

And Sir Richard Dunn, K.C.B., shook hands with Charles Knight, A.B.

"I won't forget this," he said huskily. He felt like Mahomet with his first disciple. "And now, in confidence," said the admiral, "I tell you that I mean to have Simpson's job by the time we're off the Horn."

"Good for you," said Knight. "Oh, he kicked me somethin' cruel the time him and me had a turn-up. Give it him, old man. And here's a tip for you. If you get him down, keep him down. Don't forget he kicked you, too."

"I don't forget," said Sir Richard—"I don't forget, by any means."

Yet he did his duty like a man. Though many things were strange to him, he tumbled to them rapidly. One of his fads had been doing ornamental work even when he was an admiral, and he put fresh "pointing" on the poop ladder rails for Blaker in a way that brought everyone to look at it. There was no one on board who could come within sight of him at any fancy work, and this so pleased Simpson that the admiral never had a cross word till they were south of the Horn. Then by chance the mate and the captain had a few words which ended in Simpson getting much the worst of the talk. As luck would have it, the admiral was the handiest to vent his spite on, and Simpson caught him a smack on the side of his head that made him see stars.

"Don't stand listenin' there to what don't concern you, you damned lazy hound," he said. And when the admiral picked himself off the deck, Simpson made a rush for him. The admiral dodged him and shot up the poop ladder. He took off his cap to the captain, while Simpson foamed on the main-deck and called him in vain. At any other time Blaker would have gone for the seaman who dared to escape a thrashing for the moment by desecrating the poop, but now he was willing to annoy Simpson.

"Well, what do you want?" he roared.

The admiral made a really elegant bow.

"Well, sir, I wanted to know whether Western Ocean custom goes here. I've been told that if I can thrash your mate, I shall have his job. They say forward that that's your rule, and if so, sir, I should like your permission to send Mr. Simpson forward and take his place."

There was something so open and ingenuous in the admiral that Captain Blaker, for the first time on record, burst into a shout of laughter.

"Do you hear, Mr. Simpson?" he inquired genially.

"Send him down, sir," said Simpson.

"Are you sure you can pound him?"

"Kick him off the poop, sir."

The admiral spoke anxiously.

"I'm a first-class navigator, sir. Is it a bargain?"

And Blaker, who had never liked Simpson, laughed till he cried.

"Are you willing to stake everything on your fightin' abilities, Mr. Simpson?"

And when Simpson said "Aye" through his teeth, the admiral jumped down on the main-deck.

Now, according to all precedents, the fight should have been long and arduous, with varying fortunes. But the admiral never regarded precedents, and inside of ten seconds Mr. Simpson was lying totally insensible under the spare topmast. To encounter the admiral's right was to escape death by a hair's-breadth, and it took Charles Simpson, Able Seaman (*vice* Mr. Simpson, Chief Officer), two hours and a quarter to come to.

"And I thot he could fight," said the disgusted skipper. "Come right up, Mr. What's-your-name; you're the man for me. There ain't no reason for you to trouble about my second mate, for Simpson could lay him out easy. All I ask of you is to work the whole crowd up good."

And Blaker rubbed his hands. Like Simpson at the fight between the admiral and Knight, he did not know when he had enjoyed himself more. He improved the occasion by going below and getting far too much to drink, as was his custom. And the promoted admiral took charge of the deck.

"Ability tells anywhere," said Sir Richard Dunn. "I

didn't rise in the service for nothing. Ship me where you like, and I'll come to the top. If I don't take this hooker into New York as captain and master, I'll die in the attempt."

He had quite come to himself and was beginning to enjoy himself. His natural and acquired authority blossomed wonderfully when he took on the new job, and as Blaker never swore, the admiral's gift of language was a great vicarious satisfaction to him. Wiggins accepted the situation without a murmur. Even Simpson himself bore no malice when his supplanter not only showed none, but after knocking the bosun's head against a bollard, gave his place to the former mate. Though he kept the men working and got the last ounce out of them, none of them were down on him.

"I tell you he's an admiral, sure," they said.

"He's got all the ways of one, I own," said Bill, an old man-o'-war's man. "I spoke to an admiral myself once, or rather he spoke to me."

"What did he say?" asked the rest of his watch.

"He said," replied Bill proudly—"he upped and said, 'You cross-eyed son of a dog, if you don't jump I'll bash the ugly head off of you.' And you bet I jumped. Oh, he's all the ways of *some* admirals, he has."

"Well, admiral or none," said the rest of the crowd, "things goes on pleasanter than they done when you was mate, Simpson."

And Simpson grunted.

Nothing of great interest happened till they were well east of the Horn and hauled up for the northward run. And then Blaker took to religion (or what he called religion) and rum in equally undiluted doses.

"I'm a miserable sinner, I am," he said to the admiral, "but all the same, I'll do my duty to the crowd."

He called them aft and preached to them for two hours. And when one man yawned, he laid him out with a well-directed belaying pin. The next day, when it breezed up heavily and they were shortening sail, he called all hands down from aloft on the ground that their souls were of more importance than the work in hand.

"Come down on deck, you miserable sinners," said Blaker through a speaking trumpet. His voice rose triumphantly above the roar of the gale. "Come down on deck and listen to me. For though I'm a miserable sinner, too, there's some hopes for me, and for you there's none unless you mend your ways, in accordance with what I'm telling you."

Even with the speaking trumpet he could hardly make himself heard over the roar of the increasing gale and the thunderous slatting of the topsails in the spilling-lines.

"Don't you think, sir, that they'd better make the topsails fast before you speak to them?" said the admiral.

"No, I don't," replied Blaker—"not much I don't, not by a jugful. For if one of 'em went overboard, I'd be responsible before the throne. And don't you forget it."

"Damme, he's mad," said Sir Richard—"mad as a March hare. She'll be shaking the sticks out of her soon."

He leant over the break of the poop, and called up Wiggins.

Wiggins came up, as Blaker roared his text through the trumpet.

"Will you stand by me, Mr. Wiggins, if I knock him down and take command?"

"I will; but mind his gun," said Wiggins. "When he's very bad, he'll shoot."

It was not any fear of Blaker's six-shooter that made the admiral hesitate. To take the command, even from a madman, at sea is a ticklish task and may land a man in gaol, for all his being a shanghaied admiral.

"I tell you, Mr. Wiggins, that Simpson is a good man. I'll bring him aft again."

And Wiggins made no objection when Simpson was called up by the admiral.

"Mr. Simpson," said the mate, "this is getting past a joke. Have you any objection to taking on your old job if I secure this preaching madman and take command?"

Simpson was "full up" of the foc'sle, and as he had a very wholesome admiration for the admiral, he was by no means loth to return to his old quarters.

"I'm with you, sir. In another quarter of an hour we shall have the sticks out of her."

And still Blaker bellowed scripture down the wind. He was still bellowing, though what he bellowed wasn't scripture, when Simpson and Wiggins took him down below after five minutes of a row in which the deposed captain showed something of his ancient form as the terror of the Western Ocean. As they went, the admiral, now promoted to being captain of a Cape Horner, picked up the battered speaking trumpet and wiped some blood from his face, which had been in collision.

"Up aloft with you and make those topsails fast," he roared. "Look alive, men, look alive!"

And they did look alive, for "Dicky" Dunn never needed a speaking trumpet in any wind that ever blew. When things were snugged down and the *California* was walking north at an easy but tremendous gait, he felt like a man again. He turned to Simpson and Wiggins with a happy smile.

"Now we're comfortable, and things are as they should be, Mr. Simpson, let the men have a tot of grog. And how's Mr. Blaker?"

"Wa'al," said Simpson cheerfully, "when we left him he warn't exactly what you would call religious nor resigned."

But if Blaker was not happy, the admiral was thoroughly delighted.

"Now you see what I said was true," he declared at dinner that night; "if I hadn't been an admiral and a man born to rise, how could I have been shipped on board this ship as a foremast hand and come to be captain in six weeks? I'll be bound you never heard of a similar case, Mr. Simpson."

And Simpson never had.

"Was it Shanghai Smith, do you think, as put you here?" he asked.

The admiral had heard of Shanghai Smith in the foc'sle.

"When I get back I'll find out," he said. "And if it was, I'll not trouble the law, Mr. Simpson. I never allow any man to handle me without getting more than even."

"You don't," said Simpson. If his manner was dry, it was sincere.

"But I don't bear malice afterwards. Your health, Mr. Simpson. This kind of trade breeds good seamen, after all. But you are all a trifle rough."

Simpson explained that they had to be.

"When the owners' scheme is to have one man do three men's work, they have to get men who will make 'em do it. And when the owners get a bad name and their ships a worse, then men like Shanghai Smith have to find us crews. If you could get back to San Francisco and hammer an owner, some of us would be obliged to you, sir."

"Ah, when I get back!" said the admiral. "This will be a remarkable yarn for me to tell, Mr. Simpson. I still feel in a kind of dream. Would you oblige me by going to Mr. Blaker and telling him that if he continues to hammer at that door I'll have the hose turned on him."

And when Simpson went to convey this message, the

admiral put his feet on the table and indulged in a reverie.

"I'll make a note about Shanghai Smith, and settle with him in full. But I shall rise higher yet. I know it's in me. Steward!"

"Yes, sir," said the steward.

"I think I'll have some grog."

He drank to the future of Admiral Sir Richard Dunn, master of the *California*.

8 *Master in Sail*

JAMES S. LEARMONT

O N the 10th March 1905 at 8 p.m. we passed between Flores and Corvo of the Western Islands. (I prefer this name to Azores as it was the old sea term, just as to seamen the North Atlantic is the Western Ocean.) The lights in the houses ashore were quite plain. Next day the weather was distinctly bad and blowing hard from the W.S.W. We were in company with the Italian ship *Australia* for part of the day, but left her astern.

For the next few days we ran dead before the gale and the mountainous seas, under main lower topsail, fore upper topsail with halyards eased, fore lower topsail and foresail, with all sheets eased off to make the sails give lifting power, driving-power being in this case unnecessary. The wind and squalls were terrific at times, the sea was high but it was running true. I kept her running before it, with two hands at the wheel all the time. She was running with her decks constantly full of water from rail to rail. When the watches relieved they did so on the poop after a careful count in case any had been lost on the way aft by getting jammed under the spare spars. Following a very heavy sea breaking aboard I noticed that the big teak-wood ladder had been washed from its sockets and was hanging half over the rail. The half-caste jumped to get it but I called him back saying, "If you go down there you'll go overboard." I turned and walked aft, only to hear a yell, "Come, youse fellows, get this ladder!" He had it and was floating it back.

We passed many ships lying hove to; it was very difficult to pick them up, when they happened to be in the trough of the sea at the same time as ourselves, for they had little or no canvas set. Many times, the mate approached me about the fore upper topsail, would he take it in? I replied by asking him another question: "Can you furl it?" As he was doubtful I said I might as well let it blow out of the ropes as lose it in an attempt to furl it. The lifeboats were lifted from their chocks through a heavy sea and washed up against the standard compass, damaging it, so that we had to rely on the two steering compasses. These were not of much use for navigation as they were in close proximity to the big steel wheelhouse. It was not so much a case of steering a definite course as of keeping her dead before the wind and sea as best we could; from welcome glimpses of the Pole star I knew we were making about E.N.E. but I could only guess our position.

On the afternoon of 15th March I did notice a change in the colour of the sea and this told me that we were in Soundings. We were on the shelf on which our islands stand. The same evening the weather moderated slightly and a wedge of clear sky broke out south and west of me. With a good horizon there was Sirius giving me a chance to take a sight for latitude. Running to get my sextant I told my wife to stand by the chronometers ready to take the time. I obtained an observation of Sirius and to my great joy Jupiter broke out west of me, and I got two observations for longitude.

Soon I had worked out the three sights. Returning to the poop I told the mate that when I had taken the observations we were twenty miles from the Bishop Rock Light on the Scillies and ordered him to go to the mizzen topsail yard to see if he could pick it up. Looking at me, he said, very respectfully and quietly, "Captain, you are tired out, you have been on this poop almost continuously for five days and nights. At 8 p.m. tonight it will be only five days since we passed between Flores and Corvo." I replied, "Lanchberry, they are good sights. Go ahead and have a look." Away he went and after having a look around came down, shaking his head and saying he could not see anything, repeating, "Five days from the Western Islands to Scillies, she couldn't do it." As he spoke I, still convinced that my sights were good, was looking in the direction where I was expecting to pick up the light. It was growing dark, and there flashed the welcome light; pointing it out to the mate I said, "There it is," and he exclaimed "My God!" I firmly believe that he had done his best to pick up that light but he went on his mission believing that it could not possibly be there.

Next morning we signalled Prawle Point. My father, now partially retired, happened to be in Liverpool ship-keeping with Captain Jenkins from home, and my owner, knowing that he was there, went down to inform him that I had passed Prawle. After thanking him he said, "He will not have to whistle for wind tonight," to which the owner replied, "It will be a fair wind any-way." This reply amused my father.

From Prawle I set a course to pass well clear of Port-land Bill; by this time the weather had moderated to a smart whole sail breeze and we were making about ten knots with dry decks and everything going pleasantly. We had been brought safely through a series of hard gales and now we were in Channel. My wife was near-ing her time for another child and I had hopes that we would be in Hamburg before the baby was born. In that heavy weather she had fallen and got a knocking about that could not be helped.

As we neared Portland Bill the wind died away and started to back from the westward towards the south. I was below and heard the second mate giving the orders

MY FAVOURITE SEA STORIES

to cant the yards. After reading my barometer which was still very low, I went on deck. The wind still freshening and still backing to the southward I ordered the second mate to brace her up and haul his wind. This would mean that we, instead of steering a Channel course, were now heading towards the French coast. As my wife was now approaching labour, I was up and down quite a lot.

All plain sail being set and the wind freshening, I, determined to get as far to windward as possible before the sea rose, drove her with royals set until the lee rail was under water. It was soon after that the steward came up telling me that my wife wanted me; a further stage in her labour had arrived and it was such that I must be in constant attendance. Calling the mate, for it was the dog watch and he was free, I told him to furl royals, mainsail and light head sails. Still heading south and east we stood towards France, smoothing our water all the time. We were now using the French lights for navigational purposes. The wind had increased to gale force but we had furled our topgallant sails and the mizzen upper topsail.

I had two very difficult jobs on hand, but everything was going as well as could be expected. With a fix of the lights of Cape Barfleur and the Casquets we were able to bear away up Channel. My action in hauling my wind early was now justifying itself for the southerly gale had not caught us on a lee shore, which would have been the case had we taken the usual Channel course nearer the English coast. While the mate was on deck during the 8 to 12 watch I felt I could relax regarding the ship, for he was a first-rate seaman and officer; I had plenty to occupy my mind below.

The second mate took over at midnight and shortly after 2 a.m. he called me, saying that he had noted a slight clearing in the west where the stars had broken out. The barometer was inclined to rise. I could not leave my wife to go on deck so I went along to call the mate. I found him on his settee asleep; he had lain down "all standing," fully clothed, with his oilskin coat, sou'wester and sea boots on. Rousing him I told him to go on deck and get the yards in before the wind jumped. Taking him towards the saloon so that he could reach the poop that way I gave him a good "second mate's nip" of neat whisky. He, to my surprise, removed a huge quid of tobacco from his mouth, drank the whisky and went on deck. I had already told him that he could keep her away for Dungeness. He had just finished squaring her in when the wind, in a fierce hail squall, jumped into the westward. I could hear the lumps of ice hitting the poop deck, but we were all right. She was now away before the gale, scudding up Channel.

In the morning, as we were now in narrow waters I came on deck about 7 a.m. We passed close to Dungeness and were now making sail; the royals were set although it was blowing hard. As we passed Dover we hoisted the signal letters for Lloyds Signal Station, and at about the same time I picked up the South Goodwin Light vessel. I now let her go off until the lightship was well on our port bow.

A heavy squall was coming over the Dover cliffs, and calling out for another hand to the wheel I gave the order, "Stand-by the royal halyards." The squall hit her and I yelled, "Lower away." Seeing that she had the full weight of the squall I ordered them to hold on as the royals were safer half set than on the lifts and beating in the wind. The sea was high and she was running with decks full up. My main concern was the steering, as the dreaded Goodwin Sands were not far distant; I was not concerned if she yawed to the southward as there was plenty of sea room that way. It was high water at Dover, the tide was in our favour and under the press of canvas the *Brenda* was going over the ground at a speed of at least 18 knots. When the squall cleared we were past the North Goodwin; we hadn't seen the South or East Goodwins in passing them. After setting the course I handed her over to the mate and went below. Three hours later the baby girl was born. All was well and I was grateful.

9   *Rounding the Horn*

JOHN MASEFIELD

Then came the cry of "Call all hands on deck!"
The Dauber knew its meaning; it was come:
Cape Horn, that tramples beauty into wreck,
And crumples steel and smites the strong man dumb.
Down clattered flying kites and staysails: some
Sang out in quick, high calls: the fair-leads skirled,
And from the south-west came the end of the
    world. . . .

"Lay out!" the Bosun yelled. The Dauber laid
Out on the yard, gripping the yard, and feeling
Sick at the mighty space of air displayed
Below his feet, where mewing birds were wheeling.
A giddy fear was on him; he was reeling.
He bit his lip half through, clutching the jack.
A cold sweat glued the shirt upon his back.

The yard was shaking, for a brace was loose.
He felt that he would fall; he clutched, he bent,
Clammy with natural terror to the shoes
While idiotic promptings came and went.
Snow fluttered on a wind-flaw and was spent;
He saw the water darken. Someone yelled,
"Frap it; don't stay to furl! Hold on!" He held.

Darkness came down—half darkness—in a whirl;
The sky went out, the waters disappeared.
He felt a shocking pressure of blowing hurl

The ship upon her side. The darkness speared
At her with wind; she staggered, she careered,
Then down she lay. The Dauber felt her go;
He saw his yard tilt downwards. Then the snow

Whirled all about—dense, multitudinous, cold—
Mixed with the wind's one devilish thrust and shriek,
Which whiffled out men's tears, deafened, took hold,
Flattening the flying drift against the cheek.
The yards buckled and bent, man could not speak.
The ship lay on her broadside; the wind's sound
Had devilish malice at having got her downed.

         *   *   *

How long the gale had blown he could not tell,
Only the world had changed, his life had died.
A moment now was everlasting hell.
Nature an onslaught from the weather side,
A withering rush of death, a frost that cried,
Shrieked, till he withered at the heart; a hail
Plastered his oilskins with an icy mail . . .

"Up!" yelled the Bosun; "up and clear the wreck!"
The Dauber followed where he led: below
He caught one giddy glimpsing of the deck
Filled with white water, as though heaped with snow.
He saw the streamers of the rigging blow
Straight out like pennons from the splintered mast,
Then, all sense dimmed, all was an icy blast

Roaring from nether hell and filled with ice,
Roaring and crashing on the jerking stage,
An utter bridle given to utter vice,
Limitless power mad with endless rage
Withering the soul; a minute seemed an age.
He clutched and hacked at ropes, at rags of sail,
Thinking that comfort was a fairy-tale

Told long ago—long, long ago—long since
Heard of in other lives—imagined, dreamed—
There where the basest beggar was a prince
To him in torment where the tempest screamed,
Comfort and warmth and ease no longer seemed
Things that a man could know: soul, body, brain,
Knew nothing but the wind, the cold, the pain.

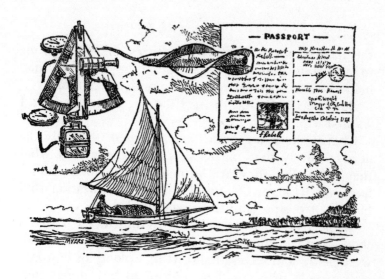

10   *The Man who Made his own Passport*

FRED REBELL

I WAS born in Latvia. Latvia was then (before the Great War) under Russian rule. Military Service was compulsory. Pacifism working strongly in me, I decided I would not serve. So, when my time came for enlistment, I dodged the Frontier Guards, and crossed into Germany.

Liberty was a holy word for me: an intense passion: and I had fled from my homeland to find her. To Germany. The young fool! She did not dwell in Germany. Imperial Germany was no "land of the free": it was no better than Tsarist Russia, as I soon found out. For instance, no one could get employment there without showing his passport.

So I went to the Russian Consul: begged him for a passport with tears in my eyes. But he would not give it me: he said he could not give a passport to a deserter.

But moved, apparently, by my distress, he directed me to a certain religious organization, saying they had helped many a young man in a position like mine.

But I did not go to them. I did not want charity: I wanted a passport.

Charitable organizations are supposed to supply the needy: surely that means supplying them with what they need. But they are limited in their ideas, and I have yet to learn of any charitable organization that hands out passports to those who need them.

While I was pondering over this difficulty I passed a shop where furniture and all sorts of household goods were being sold second-hand. It had plenty of custom: poor people who could not afford to buy things new thronged it. "Well," I thought, "if a second-hand bed is good enough, why not a second-hand passport?" True, it would not be smart and shiny like a new one: but a new one soon gets smudged and dirty from living in your pocket and being thumbed by greasy officials: and then, what is the difference? True, it would be nicer to have a new one; but if I could not get a new one, why be squeamish?

In Hamburg in those days there was a public-house called the *Verbrechers Kneipe*, which means "criminals' pub". I soon found out that this was the chief Exchange of second-hand passports and documents of all kinds. Before long, I found there a passport which I could have at a bargain-price—only half a dollar. It was a bit grubby, but it appeared good enough to get me a job: so I bought it.

However, it turned out not such a good bargain as it looked. It was like this. I had decided on going to sea, so as to see something of the world—and perhaps even to find somewhere a country not under the Rule of Paper. But to go to sea, you needed as well as a passport a seafaring permit. So I went to the German Maritime Office to get one; and, of course, showed them my passport, and claimed the name on it. Had I been to sea before? they asked me. "No." So then the official started looking in a great ledger.

"What!" he said. "What do you mean by saying you have never been to sea, and right here are entries for three different voyages on three different ships?"

So now I saw why that passport had been so cheap! "Paul Sproge" (the man I was now) must have been a seaman, and have deserted his ship somewhere, so losing his seaman's book (which, of course, the Captain keeps until you are discharged). No wonder he had been so willing to sell his name and his passport, seeing all they were really good for was to get one into gaol!

"I lost the book," I said.

"Then don't come here telling lies," shouted the official, "or I will fetch the police."

Well, I thought, as I walked out, that is just too bad. But after all this is a good passport: it only wants a minor adjustment. It only wants a new name on it. You don't throw away your watch because one of the hands is bent, you fix a new hand. So I went to a chemist and bought some stuff, and soon the old name was gone.

That was the end of "Paul Sproge." When a young applicant for a seaman's book next appeared at the Maritime Office, the name on his passport was Fred Rebell. "Fred Rebell" could not have three ships registered against him, because he had only been born half an hour before. The youngest seaman in all Hamburg. They gave "Fred Rebell" the seafaring permit all right, and it was not long before he got a job.

You think I did wrong? What wrong had I done? Papers do not mean anything, anyway. A man means something, and work means something. If a government is so crazy that it will not let a man have work unless he has got papers, then it is only rational to humour that crazy government like you humour any other sort of lunatic. Suppose you were sitting in a room and a crazy man jumped in at the window. "Are you Julius Caesar?" he says. "If you are not I will kill you."— "Certainly I am Julius Caesar," you would answer, edging for the door. And would your conscience worry you for that? Well, I was in the same position—up against something crazy that was stronger than I. "Certainly," I said, "I am Fred Rebell. It must be so, because it is written on my passport."

—Reader, you do not often get a moral at the beginning of a story: but I am going to give you one now. (Maybe there are other morals, but I will save them for later.) All those big militarist countries with their emperors and their thrones and their armies and their guns and their frontiers and their frontier-guards and their officials, and above all their passports: see them on one side, and see me on the other, a young idealist student who had run away from home and lived with the lowest of the low. I ask you, which would you say was the stronger if you had seen us then? Which looked as if it would last the longer? And yet, where are those empires today? Under the sod. And where am I? Here, and not only a living man, but today a happy man—which is a lot more than I was then.

Armed with his self-provided papers, Fred Rebell got himself jobs in ships' stokeholds. It was easier to find employment there than on deck, for the work was harder. He became a competent ship's fireman. In 1907, he wanted to get to Australia—right out of Europe, begin again. He stowed away in a steamship, reported to the Chief Engineer not the Master, for he knew that the Chief could use a good fireman: and so it was. Landing in Australia with £16 he found plenty of work, clearing virgin land, saw-milling, the toughest work of

*this world, like ship's firing. He saved £500, took a
"selection", made a farm out of it, did well: then lost
the lot in the great depression. His attempts at family
life failed too. He decided to go to America. How?
Officials refused him a visa.*

So he would sail there himself. He did.

For twenty pounds, I bought a second-hand eighteen-
foot C.B. sloop, of the type that has been perfected for
racing in the sheltered waters of Sydney Harbour. She
was not decked in, of course; and I could not afford to
deck her. Her draught was only eighteen inches and her
free-board twenty inches.

In that boat I intended to sail to America. Was ever
an ocean voyage projected in a more unsuitable craft?

Built for speed and lightness, it was plain that her
hull would never stand the battering of big seas. So I
strengthened it, by doubling the number of her ribs and
by fixing an outside keel. As for shelter, the best I could
contrive was a canvas hood amidships (which would at
least keep the spray off me). And I enlarged my sail.

But buying and improving the boat was not the only
expense entailed. This voyage might take me a year,
and I had to provision her. True, I could replenish my
stores at islands on the way: so I provisioned her with
only six months' supply of dry food. I packed it all in
paraffin cans, fitted with screw caps: plenty of flour,
that is to say; rice, wheat, pearl-barley, peas, beans,
sugar, semolina, rolled oats, and powdered skim milk.
Also dried fruit, potatoes, onions, lime-juice, olive oil,
treacle, and yeast. I also took on board thirty gallons of
water, in tins and drums which I had lined with asphalt
(and it kept remarkably well like that). But because I
was provisioning her at the minimum cost, I could allow
myself no luxuries. I took no tinned food; no tea,
tobacco, spirits, or medicines.

My rationing allowed for one and a half pounds of dried food per day, and about one-third of a gallon of water. I might, of course, hope to catch some fresh fish; and sea-water would have to serve me instead of salt.

For cooking purposes I shipped a Primus stove, a bottle of methylated, matches, and five gallons of paraffin. I also stowed on board an electric pocket-torch, my kit of carpenter's tools, paint, pitch, bits of wood, nails, and all sorts of odds and ends that I thought would come in useful on the way. The total cargo weighed, probably, half a ton.

But there are other things a mariner needs, besides a ship and food and water. He needs navigating-instruments, and charts. And these are expensive—far beyond the means of a man as hard-up as I was.

By the airs the makers of nautical instruments give themselves, you would think no one could do their work who had not been serving an apprenticeship of one hundred years! Well, I would have a try.

The most important instrument of all, of course, was the sextant, since it is with that you learn your position (when out of sight of land) from the sun and stars. It has to be extremely accurately made because the slightest fault in it may cause your computed position to be wrong by hundreds of miles. Well, the materials I used for my sextant were several pieces of hoop-iron; a Boy Scout telescope (price one shilling); an old hacksaw-blade; and a stainless steel table-knife.

I broke pieces off the table-knife, to make the mirrors. They had to be ground optically flat, which I accomplished by melting a lump of bitumen on to them for finger-grips, and by rubbing them over emery-cloth laid on a piece of plate-glass. I used three grades of emery-cloth—coarse, medium and fine—and finally I gave the steel a mirror finish by rubbing it on a damp cloth with red oxide (or jeweller's rouge).

The hacksaw-blade, of course, was for the degree-scale. I chose it because of its regularly cut teeth, and because I could bend it into an arc. I so chose the radius of the arc that two teeth made one degree. I took the temper out of the blade so that I should be able to re-shape the teeth, and for a tangent screw I took an ordinary wood-screw that would engage nicely with the hacksaw. This way, I could read the half-degrees of arc straight off the teeth of the hacksaw. But half a degree of latitude represents thirty nautical miles, and you need far greater accuracy than that. So I enlarged the head of the screw, and sub-divided its circumference by sixty. Thus I was able to read to minutes of arc off the screw-head itself (each minute corresponds to *one* nautical mile only).

That was the hardest job to make.

The next thing I needed was a chronometer. Well, I could not make a chronometer; but I bought two cheap watches (each as a check on the other) for a few shillings. I slung them in gimbals, so that the motion of the boat should not affect them.

He made a patent log, too—a device for measuring the miles sailed. For a week or two he pottered about Sydney harbour to get the feel of his craft. He read up seamanship in Sydney's Mitchell Library, and copied a few Pacific maps from an old atlas there. He bought an old work on astronomical navigation, leaving its study until he got to sea ... A demand for arrears of taxes decided his sailing-date. His few pounds could pay that demand or finance his small needs for the trans-Pacific voyage. He sailed.

I cast off, and with the faintest of breezes made my way slowly down the harbour. It was nearly noon, and for the last time I checked my sextant by the meridian altitude of the sun. It proved to be fairly accurate; my calculated position only differed by two or three miles from my known position.

Shortly after, I passed under the great harbour bridge. It was now nearly completed. Would I ever see it again, I wondered?

Had I taken any notice of evil omens, probably I should never have gone outside the Heads. For, beating down the harbour, I carried on too long on the inshore tack, and bumped a rock! First evil omen! Second, a mile or two farther down I got caught in a "buster." These "busters" are sudden squalls, and common on hot afternoons. Had I kept my eye on the shore-line I might have seen it coming, in a swirl of dust. But I was not keeping a proper look-out; and before I knew what was happening, the "buster" was on me. The sail flapped wildly, and the boat heeled over till water was pouring in over the gunwale. Then away she tore with the boom scoring the water—until I was able to get the mainsail down.

Within a few minutes the placid waters of Sydney Harbour had been whipped up into quite formidable waves. Should I run for shelter till it was over, or should I keep on?

Just then I caught sight of a little sailing dinghy, right out in the middle of the harbour, manned by two schoolboys. She was tearing along under full sail, bouncing on the waves like a kangaroo. "If those two kids have courage to carry on, so ought you," I said to myself, "in your bigger boat. If you have to run for shelter before you are even out of Sydney Harbour, what will you do if you meet a storm in the open ocean?"

So under jib alone I sailed out through the Heads. Outside there was a big swell; but my boat rode it nicely. I rode it less nicely, however: I was seasick. But that attack of seasickness only lasted half an hour;

and since then I have never been seasick in my life again.

For a long while I watched the receding shore, and as dusk was approaching I stood up in the stern: waved my hand towards the land, and sang out, "Good-bye, Australia! Good-bye, sweetheart! Good-bye for ever."

*　　*　　*

My course lay due east: and as I progressed eastward, the sun would rise and set earlier day by day. Likewise, of course, noon would come round sooner; so that on my fourth week out from Sydney it fell at 10 a.m. (by Sydney time). Now every four minutes of difference in time corresponds to one degree of longitude: so I knew that I was now thirty degrees of longitude east of Sydney.

This method of longitude computation is simple in principle: but it is not always so easy to carry out as it would appear. For in order to ascertain exactly the time at which the local noon occurs, two observations are needed: one in the morning and one in the afternoon. The sun's altitude at the time of the first observation is recorded; then a second observation is taken, to discover at what time the sun has sunk to exactly this altitude once more (noon, of course, will be the midpoint between these two times). But suppose that when the time comes for the second observation, the sky is cloudy? All chance of ascertaining your position that day has gone. And during these weeks the sky was so often cloudy that I determined to master other methods, requiring more calculation but more often practicable. By the use of tables and logarithms I learned to compute my longitude with only a single easterly or westerly observation of sun, moon or planets. For latitude, however, I still relied on the highest or noon altitude of the sun.

I had intended to call at Auckland in New Zealand: but after four weeks at sea I found I was already far to the east of it. I had missed New Zealand altogether.

It was better to miss New Zealand than to hit it. He picked up the Trade Wind and continued towards the Fijis, the rough Tasman Sea behind him. He cooked by primus, boiling cocoa, making tea, even baking a little bread and frying small fish he caught. His plans being simple worked. He saw land after 40 days.

Perhaps under the influence of land, the weather now changed. I had only forty miles to go to reach Suva: but I was making very slow progress. Other islands dotted my course: where there are islands there are reefs, and night-sailing in consequence became extremely dangerous. I began to feel the lack of sleep. I had also broken into my very last gallon of drinking-water. So presently, when I drew near a small island covered with luxuriant vegetation, I decided to call there.

I sailed round under its lee, dropped my hook, and then—so as to be able to work in to shallow water—hauled up the centre-board.

I thought it might be a bit of a job, hauling this up after it had been down for so long; but to my surprise it came up more lightly than usual. I soon discovered why. Only the top of it was still there! All the bottom part, which should have projected below the keel and acted as a fin, had carried away. So that was why my boat had sailed so badly the last few weeks! Why it had slipped so many miles to leeward, and been ready to heel over in the lightest of breezes! Disgusted, I chucked the remaining remnant of the board into the sea. Then I waded ashore, and found myself at last on solid ground.

But, solid ground? This was not solid ground! It rocked and heaved under me like a raft. With every surge of surf on the beach the whole island seemed to heave and tilt under me, so that I could barely keep my balance, and staggered like a drunken man.

Reason told me it was myself that must be afflicted in this way, and not the island. And indeed this was the case: after two months in a tossing boat I had lost my shore-legs entirely.

It was only by adopting a swaggering sailor's gait that I presently was able to get along at all.

I began to explore, traversing the shore for half a mile each way. There was no sign of human habitation anywhere, nor even of animal life. Tall coconut-trees fringed the island: and behind that fringe were gullies where a profusion of shrub, tree and creeper crowded each on one another, blotting out the blue of the sky. Amongst them I noticed pawpaw-trees and bananas with bunches of unripe fruit. A sombre shade hung over this grove, and a smell of decaying vegetation permeated the air. And a silence. Nothing stirred: a lizard scurrying out of my way, a hermit crab withdrawing into its shell, were the only bustle and tumult that the island knew.

Moreover, I found no stream, nor any sign of drinking-water. So I picked up a few coconuts that were lying on the ground, and returned to my boat. I decided to sail round to the windward side of the island and look for a settlement. But that must wait until to-morrow: night was closing in, and the first thing was to find a safe anchorage for a proper night's rest.

I lifted my eyes towards the setting sun: and a strange sight met them. About a mile away, and as far to right and left as the eye could see, the whole horizon—just above the blue of the sea—appeared to be studded with a row of pebbles, boulders, and pillars: with here and there among them a white line of ocean rollers breaking into foam. It was the outer reef surrounding the island, now laid bare by the receding tide. How I had got inside it, I knew not: by sheer good fortune the flood tide must have carried me through some passage or over some low-lying part of it.

As I stared at this reef my eye was caught by a sail—the first I had seen since I left Australia. It grew larger: and presently through a gap in the reef a small schooner appeared, brought-to in the lagoon, and anchored. I pushed off my boat and sailed towards them; for here evidently were people who knew the place, and who could give me useful information.

She turned out to be a Chinese fishing and trading schooner of forty tons. Her crew numbered only two: and you will guess that it was only with the greatest difficulty that I was able to make myself understood by them. But when they gathered that I had come from Australia they became very interested, and indeed cordial. They had just finished their meal, but they offered me some cooked rice and tea, which I gladly accepted; and they pointed out to me a safe anchorage for the night.

What a relief it was, after all I had gone through, to be swinging gently at anchor all through the night! No worry about getting off one's course, or of running into a reef!

The first lap behind him, his sea stores replenished with bananas and papaya and his drinking-water by fresh coconuts at wayside islands, he continued on his leisurely way. Port officials disbelieved him at first, but soon learned to accept and even to admire this unusual care-free wanderer with his fantastic craft. It had brought him that far: let him go—that was their reasoning. So he sailed on. Flights of birds helped his navigation. The trade winds were easy on his sails—mostly.

He still had no passport. At Christmas Island he learned that he must present such a document, properly visaed, to enter his next stop—the Hawaiian Islands. He took steps.

So now I knew what I could expect myself. It was plainly necessary that I should have a passport.

But why should I apply to any Government for one? I ruled my own life: no Government ruled me. I had made my own sextant and other necessities for the voyage: why should I not issue my own passport? So that is what I proceeded to do; and without charging myself any fee drew up the document.

I was not prepared, however, to sail back to Suva in order to have this document *visé* by the American Consul there—even if he had been willing to attach his visa to such an unusual document. I would sail on, and take my chance. But since one visa might be expected to attract others—like sheep going through a gap in a hedge—I started my collection with the only visa there available—that of M. Paul Rougier, as representing the Government of Christmas Island.

So, on the morning of 25th August, I took my departure from Christmas Island. I had now another long run ahead of me—the twelve-hundred-mile run to Honolulu. I half thought of calling at Fanning Island on the way—it is only about one hundred and fifty miles north-west from Christmas Island. But corrosion had put my taffrail-log altogether out of commission, and, between my "fixes" by the sun, I had no way of checking the distance run. Moreover, I was being borne northward by a strong current, and I soon found that I had been carried past that island.

So he continued quietly towards Hawaii.

My taffrail-log was now useless: I could no longer rely on my watches: but neither of these things caused me much worry. The Sandwich Islands are large, and there was little likelihood of my missing them. My course was now due north: with a fair wind, I could keep to it pretty accurately: and noon altitudes of the sun, by giving me my latitude, gave me also exactly the progress I was making.

I had by now acquired a contemplative mind, and the three weeks of this passage passed quickly enough. Night after night the Southern Cross ever more closely hugged the horizon, and at last disappeared altogether as the Pole Star came into view. Once more the sky was lit by those familiar northern constellations that I had not seen for so many years.

It was on the morning of the 15th September that I sighted Hawaii, about forty miles to starboard. As I approached it, however, the high mountain completely choked the breeze; and though there was a heavy swell coming round each end of the island, I had not a breath to steady me. For nearly a day my boat lay there, rocking most uncomfortably. When at last a blow did set in it carried me to Lanai, another of the Hawaian group. About twelve miles south of Lanai I again got becalmed —again on account of a mountain blocking the Trade Wind. Every now and then there would be a breath or two; I would hoist sail and make a few miles' progress, only to find myself drifting back again in the ensuing calm. In desperation I tried rowing, but after an hour's exhausting work I seemed to be doing no good: so I gave it up as a bad job.

Then, as if to try my patience still further, one tiresome little harbinger of land flew out to meet me. It was a black stinging ant, and after the long aerial voyage it had accomplished—when you would have expected it to have little thought for anything but rest—what must it do, but set to work immediately on landing at crawling inside my shirt and stinging me all round the waist!

Gradually, however, I did make progress, a mile or two at a time. Oahu, the island Honolulu is on, was as yet below the horizon; but now at night I could see the glow of the city lights on the clouds in the north-west.

At last, on the third day, a sharp blow set in, and within twenty-four hours I was just opposite Honolulu harbour, where I dropped anchor for the night.

Early next morning my yellow flag was up, and I watched till noon; but nobody seemed to take any notice: so I raised anchor and sailed right in.

I had been twenty-six days on the way from Christmas Island: and because of the great number of drinking coconuts I had been supplied with my water consumption for this passage had amounted to only six gallons! Less than a quart a day. I had still about thirty gallons of water in my tanks, and enough food for six months. Even if I had missed the Sandwich Islands, I still should have made the American coast without much trouble: and I could hardly have missed *that*.

Luckily during the run my watch had kept a fairly even rate, so I was barely thirty miles out in my longitude reckoning.

There was difficulty at Honolulu. After all, Wanderer Rebell was unique.

The second day I was in port, an officer from the Immigration Department asked me to call at his office.

The first thing he wanted to know was whether I had a passport.

"Sure," said I, and produced the one I had written out for myself—bearing as its only visa the official stamp of M. Rougier, affixed at Christmas Island.

Needless to say, this document rather flummoxed the Immigration officer. "This is not an *official* passport," he complained.

"What makes a passport official?" I asked him.

"Well, it must be issued by a man's government," he said.

"I am my own government," I answered: "and I issued myself this passport, so it is official."

"Well, then," he said, "it has not got an American Visa."

"That is true," I answered. "Granted, I have omitted taking the trifling trouble of travelling three thousand miles for the privilege of presenting an American Consul with ten dollars. I admit it. But the point is, what are you going to do about it? It is the only passport I have. If you will not accept it you have no alternative but to push me back into the sea."

This made him uncomfortable. "No," he said: "we won't do that."

It ended with their taking from me a statement long enough to make a three-volume biography: my nationality, pedigree, relations, education, occupation, previous residences, intentions—and what not. But they did not push me back into the sea.

No, they did not push him back into the sea. Nobody pushed him into the sea. Fred Rebell stayed five weeks in Honolulu, then sailed the long, rough leg to the Californian coast—unperturbed as ever, coping with each day and its problems as they came, steadily reading through H. G. Wells' "Outline of History" as day followed day and the 18-foot harbour craft slipped or rolled or leapt along. It was autumn then. He bounced through several gales.

On January 7, 1933, Rebel Rebell and his £20 skiff slid quietly into San Pedro Harbour, California, a year and a week out of Sydney, N.S.W.—a remarkable feat by an extraordinary man. He threw over a small anchor, thanked God, and turned in.

Note: All links in this story were written by the Editor.

11 *A Hot Cargo*

DAVID W. BONE

SHOREFOLK can have but a hazy idea of all that it means to the deep-water sailor when at last, after long voyaging, the port of his destination heaves in sight. For months he has been penned up on shipboard, the subject of a discipline more strict than that in any way of life ashore. The food, poor in quality, and of meagre allowance at the best, has become doubly distasteful to him. The fresh water has nearly run out, and the red rusty sediment of the tank bottoms has a nauseating effect and does little to assuage the thirst engendered by salt rations. Shipmates have told and retold their yarns, discussions now verge perilously on a turn of fisticuffs. He is wearying of sea life, is longing for a change, for a break in the monotony of day's work and watch-keeping, of watch-keeping and day's work.

A welcome reaction comes on the day when he is

ordered to put the harbour gear in readiness. Generally he has only a hazy notion of the ship's position (it is sea fashion to keep that an Officers' secret), and the rousing up of the long idle anchor chains and tackle is his first intimation that the land is near, that any day may now bring the shore to view, that soon he will be kicking his heels in a sailor-town tavern, washing off his "salt casing" with lashings of the right stuff.

This was in part our case when we were a hundred and forty days out from the Clyde. The food was bad and short allowance; the key of the pump was strictly guarded, but we had excitement enough and to spare, for, six days before our "landfall," the bo'sun discovered fire in the forehold that had evidently been smouldering for some time, was deep-seated, and had secured a firm hold.

It was difficult to get at the fire on account of the small hatchway, and notwithstanding the laboured efforts of all hands, we were at last obliged to batten the hatches down and to trust to a lucky "slant" to put us within hail of assistance. The water which we had so fruitlessly poured below had all to be pumped out again to get the ship in sailing trim; and heart-breaking work it was, with the wheezy old pump sucking every time the ship careened to leeward. Anxiety showed on all faces, and it was with great relief that, one day at noon, we watched the Mate nailing a silver dollar to the mizzenmast. The dollar was his who should first sight the distant shore.

We held a leading wind from the norrard, and when, on the afternoon of a bright day, we heard the glad shout from the fore-tops'l yard—"Land-oh"—we put a hustle on our movements, and, light at heart, found excuse to lay aloft to have a faraway look at God's good earth again. It was the Farallone Islands we had made— thirty miles west from the Golden Gate—a good landfall.

Dutch John was the lucky man to see it first, and we gave him a cheer as he laid aft to take the dollar off the mast.

In the second dog-watch we hung about the decks discussing prospective doings when we set foot ashore, and those who had been in 'Frisco before formed centres of inquiry and importance. From the bearing of the land, we expected orders to check in the yards, but, greatly to our surprise, the Mate ordered us to the lee fore-brace, and seemed to be unable to get the yards far enough forrard to please him. When Wee Laughlin came from the wheel at eight bells, we learned that the ship was now heading to the nor'east, and away from our port; and the old hands, with many shakings of the head, maintained that some tricky game was afoot. The Old Man and the Mate were colloguing earnestly at the break of the poop; and Jones, who went aft on a pretence of trimming the binnacle, reported that the Old Man was expressing heated opinions on the iniquity of salvage. At midnight we squared away, but as we approached the land the wind fell light and hauled ahead. Wonder of wonders! This seemed to please the Captain hugely, and his face beamed like a nor'west moon every time he peered into the compass.

Dawn found us well to the norrard of the islands, and close-hauled, standing into the land. From break of day all hands were busy getting the anchors cleared and the cables ranged. Some were engaged painting out the rusty bits on the starboard topside. A "work-up" job they thought it was until the Mate ordered them to leave the stages hanging over the water abreast of the fore-hatch. Here the iron plating was hot, the paint was blistered off, and every time the ship heeled over there was an unmistakable *sssh* as the water lapped the heated side. This, and the smell of hot iron, was all there was to tell of our smouldering coal below, but 'Frisco men from the Water Front are sharp as ferrets, and very little would give them an inkling of the state of affairs. Presently we raised the land broad on the port bow, and two of us were perched on the fore-to'gal'nt yard to look out for the pilot schooner; or, if luck was in our way, a tow-boat. The land became more distinct as the day wore on, and the bearing of several conspicuous hills gave the Captain the position he sought. Before noon, we reported smoke ahead, and the Mate, coming aloft with his telescope, made out the stranger to be a tow-boat, and heading for us. We were called down from aloft, and the ship was put about.

We were now, for the second time, heading away from our port; and when the Mate set us to slap the paint on the burned patch, we understood the Old Man's manoeuvre, which had the object of preventing the tow-boat from rounding to on our starboard side. Her skipper would there have assuredly seen evidences of our plight, and would not have been slow to take advantage of it.

The tug neared us rapidly (they lose no time on the Pacific slope), and the Captain recognised her as the *Active*.

"She's one of Spreckels' boats," said he, shutting his glass. "Cutbush runs her, an' he's a dead wide one. If he smells a rat, Mister, we'll be damned lucky if we get into harbour under a couple o' thousand."

We were all excited at the game, though it mattered little to us what our owners paid, as long as we got out of our hot corner. Straight for us he came, and when he rounded our stern and lay up on the lee quarter, the bo'sun voiced the general opinion that the Old Man had done the trick.

"Morn, Cap.! Guess ye've bin a long time on th' road," sang out the tow-boat's skipper, eyeing our rusty side and grassy counter.

"Head winds," said the Old Man, "head winds, an' no luck this side o' th' Horn."

"Ye're a long way to th' norrard, Cap. Bin havin' thick weather outside?"

"Well, not what ye might call thick, but musty, these last few days. We were lookin' to pick up the Farallones." (The unblushing old Ananias!)

There ensued a conversation about winds and weather, ships and freights, interspersed with the news of five months back. The talk went on, and neither seemed inclined to get to business. At last the two-boat man broke the ice.

Waal, Cap., I reckon ye don't want t' stay here all day. Wind's easterly inside, an' there ain't none too much water on th' bar. Ye'd better give us yer hawser 'n let's git right along."

"Oh! no hurry, Capt'in; there's no hurry. What's a day here or there when ye'r well over the hundreds? I can lay up to th' pilot ground on th' next tack . . . Ye'll be wantin' a big figure from here, an' my owners won't stand a long pull."

"Only six hundred, Cap., only six hundred, with your hawser."

The Old Man started back in amazement.

"Six hundred dollars, Capt'in? Did you say six hundred? Holy smoke! I don't want t' buy yer boat, Capt'in. . . . Six hundred—well, I'm damned. Loose them royals, Mister! Six hundred, no damn fear!"

Quickly we put the royals on her, though they were little use, the wind having fallen very light. The tow-boat sheered off a bit, and her skipper watched us sheeting-home, as if it were a most interesting and uncommon sight.

He gave his wheel a spoke or two and came alongside again.

"All right, Give us yer hawser 'n I'll dock ye for five-fifty!"

The Old Man paid no attention to his request, but paced fore and aft the weather side, gazing occasionally at the lazy royals, then fixing the man at the wheel with a reproachful eye. At last he turned to leeward with a surprised expression, as if astonished to find the tow-boat still there.

"Come, Cap.! Strike it right naow! What d'ye offer? Mind the wind, as there is ov it, is due east in the Strait."

The Old Man thought carefully for quite a time. "Hundred n' fifty, 'n your hawser," he said.

The Captain of the *Active* jammed his bell rod at full speed ahead.

"Good morn, Cap.," he said. "Guess I'll see ye in 'Frisco this side o' the Noo Year." He forged rapidly ahead, and when clear of the bows took a long turn to seaward. The Mate took advantage of his being away and wiped off the paint on the burned patch, which was beginning to smell abominably. Fresh paint was hurriedly put on, and the stages were again aboard when the *Active,* finding nothing to interest her on the western horizon, returned—again to the lee quarter.

"Saay, Cap., kan't we do a deal; kan't we meet somewhere?" said Cutbush, conciliatory.

"Say five hundred or four-eighty, 'n I'll toss ye for th' hawser?"

"I can't do it, Capt'in . . . I'd lose my job if I went," (here the Old Man paused to damn the steersman's eyes, and to tell him to keep her full) "if I went to that length."

The tow-boat again sheered off and her skipper busied himself with his telescope.

"Waal, Cap., she may be a smart barque, but I'm darn ef ye can beat her through the Golden Gate the way th' wind is. Saay! Make it three-fifty? What the hell's about a fifty dollars. Darn me! I've blown that in half-hour's poker!"

"Aye, aye! That's so; but I'm no' takin' a hand in that game. Set the stays'ls, Mister, 'n get a pull on the fore 'n main sheets!"

We went about the job, and the *Active* took another turn, this time to the south'ard. Munro, aloft loosing the staysails, reported a steamer away under the land. She was sending up a dense smoke, and that caused the Old Man to account her another tow-boat out seeking.

"That'll fetch him," he said to the Mate, " 'n if he offers again I'll close. Three-fifty's pretty stiff, but we can't complain."

"Egad, no!" said the Mate; "if I'd been you I'd have closed for five hundred, an' be done with it."

"Aye, aye, no doubt! no doubt! But ye're not a Scotchman looking after his owners' interest."

Soon we saw the *Active* smoking up and coming towards us with 'a bone in her mouth'. Cutbush had seen the stranger's smoke, and he lost no time. He seemed to be heading for our starboard side and we thought the game was up; but the Old Man kept off imperceptibly, and again the tug came to port.

"Changed yer mind, Cap.? Guess I must be gwine back. Got t' take the *Drumeltan* up t' Port Costa in th' mornin'. What d'ye say t' three hundred?"

The Old Man called the Mate, and together they held a serious consultation with many looks to windward, aloft, and at the compass. The stranger was rapidly approaching, and showed herself to be a yellow-funnelled tow-boat, with a business-like foam about her bows. Spreckels' man was getting fidgety, as this was one of the opposition boats, and he expected soon to be quoting a competitive figure. To his pleased surprise, the Old Man came over to leeward, and, after a last wrangle about the hawser, took him on at the satisfactory figure of three hundred dollars.

We put about, and the Mate had another little deal in burned paint. Courses were hauled up, and the *Active* came along our starboard side to pass the towing wire aboard. The paint hid the patch, and in the manoeuvre of keeping clear of our whisker-booms, the smell escaped notice, and the marks of our distress were not noticed by the crew. We hauled the wire aboard and secured the end, and the *Active's* crew heard nothing significant in the cheer with which we set about clewing-up and furling sail.

The afternoon was far spent when we reached the pilot schooner. She was lying at anchor outside the bar, the wind having died away; and as she lifted to the swell, showed the graceful underbody of an old-time "crack". The pilot boarded us as we towed past. Scarce was he over the rail before he shouted to the Old Man, "What's the matter, Cap'n? Guess she looks 's if she had a prutty hot cargo aboard."

"Hot enough, Pilot! Hot enough, b' Goad! We've bin afire forr'ard these last seven days that we know of, and I'm no' sayin' but that I'm glad t' see th' beach again."

"Waal, that's bad, Cap'n. That's bad. Ye won't make much this trip, I guess, when the 'boys' have felt ye over." He meant when the 'Frisco sharps had got their pickings, and the Old Man chuckled audibly as he replied.

"Oh, we'll chance that—aye, we'll chance that. It's no' so bad's if Cutbush was gettin' his figger."

"What's he gettin', anyway?"

"Oh, he's doin' verra well. He's doin' verra well," said the Old Man evasively.

We were now approaching the far-famed Golden Gate, the talk of mariners on seven seas. We boys were

sent aloft to unrig the chafing gear, and took advantage
of our position and the Mate's occupation to nurse the
job, that we might enjoy the prospect. The blue head-
land and the glistening shingle of Drake's Bay to the
norrard and the high cliffs of Benita ahead; the land
stretching away south, and the light of the westing sun
on the distant hills. No wonder that when the Mate
called us down from aloft to hand flags there was much
of our work left unfinished.

At Benita Point we had a busy time signalling news
of our condition to the ship's agents at 'Frisco. After we
passed through the Narrows, we had a near view of the
wooded slopes of Sausalito, with the white-painted
houses nestling comfortably among the trees. Away to
the right the undulating plains of the Presidio reached
out to the purple haze of the distant city. The Pilot,
seeing admiration in our eyes, couldn't hold his pride,
even to us boys, and exclaimed aloud on the greatness
of the U—nited States in possessing such a seaboard.

"Saay, boys," he said. "Guess yew ain't got nothin'
like this in th' old country!'"

Young Munro, who was the nearest, didn't let the
Pilot get away with that, and he mentioned a "glint of
Loch Fyre, when the sun was in the west'ard." "And
that's only one place I'm speakin' of."

The sun was low behind us as we neared the anchorage, and a light haze softened and made even more
beautiful the outlines of the stately City. As we looked
on the shore, no one had mind of the long dreary voyage.
That was past and done. We had thought only for the
City of the West that lay before us, the dream of many
long weary nights.

But, as I gazed and turned away, I was sharply
minded of what the sea held for us. Houston had been
carried on deck, "t' see th' sichts," as he said. His stret-
cher stood near me, and the sight of his wan face brought

up the memory of bitter times "off the Horn". Of the black night when we lost Duncan! Of the day when Houston lay on the cabin floor, and the seaman-surgeon and his rude assistants buckled to "the job"! Of the screams of the tortured lad—"Let me alane! Oh, Christ! Let me al—" till kindly Mother Nature did what we had no means to do! . . .

"Man, but it was a tough job, with her rolling and pitching in the track o' th' gale!" The Old Man was telling the Pilot about it. "But there he is, noo! As sound as ye like . . . a bit weak, mebbe, but sound! . . . We'll send him t' th' hospital, when we get settled down. . . . No' that they could dae mair than I've dune." Here a smile of worthy pride. "But a ship's no' the place for scienteefic measures—stretchin', an' rubbin' an' that . . . Oh, yes! Straight? I'll bate ye he walks as straight as a serjunt before we're ready for sea again!"

As we drew on to the anchorage, a large raft-like vessel with barges in tow made out to meet us. The Old Man turned his glasses on her and gave an exclamation of satisfaction.

"Meyer's been damn smart in sending out the fire-float," he said to the Mate, adding, "Get the foreyard cock-billed, Mister; and a burton rigged to heave out the cargo as soon's we anchor. There's the tow-boat whistlin' for ye to shorten in th' hawser. Bear a hand, mind ye, for we've a tough night's work before us."

*   *   *

But all was not pleasant anticipation aboard of the screw tug *Active,* towing gallantly ahead, for Captain John Cutbush had discovered his loss, and the world wasn't big enough for his indictment of Fortune.

He had seen our flags off Benita, but had not troubled to read the message, as he saw the answering pennant flying from the Lighthouse. In scanning the anchorage for a convenient berth to swing his tow in, the fire-float caught his eye.

"Hello! somethin' afire in th' Bay!" He turned his glasses among the shipping, in search of a commotion, but all was quiet among the tall ships.

"But where's she lyin'-to fer? There ain't nothin' this side ov Alcatraz, I reckon."

Then a dread suspicion crossed his mind, that made him jump for the signal-book. He remembered the flags of our last hoist, and feverishly turned them up.

"Arrange—assistance—for—arrival."

Muttering oaths, he dropped the book and focused his glasses on the tow. The track of the fire was patent to the world now, and we were unbending the sails from the yards above the forehatch.

"She's afire right 'nuff, 'n I never cottoned. Roast me for a——. 'N that's what the downy old thief was standin' t' th' norrard for, 'n I never cottoned! 'N that's what he took me on at three hundred for, 'n Meyer's boat almost alongside. Three hundred 'n my —— hawser. Wa'al—I'm damned! The old lime juice pirate. Guess I should 'a known him for a bloody sharp when I saw Glasgow on her stern."

He stopped cursing, to blow his whistle—a signal for us to shorten in the towing hawser. In the ensuing manoeuvres he was able to relieve his feelings by criticising our seamanship; he swung us round with a vicious sheer, eased up, and watched our anchor tumbling from the bows. He gazed despairingly at his Mate, who was steering.

"Here's a ruddy mess, Gee-orge," he said. "Three thousan' dollars clean thrown away. What'll the boss say. What'll they say on th' Front?"

George cursed volubly, and expanded much valuable tobacco juice.

Here's a boomer fer th' *Examiner,* George; here's a sweet headline fer th' *Call*!

" 'Cutbush done!'

" 'Cap'n Jan Cutbush done in th' eye!'

" 'Cap'n Jan S. Cutbush, th' smartest skipper on th' Front, done in the bloody eye by a bargoo-eatin' son of a gun of a grey-headed lime-juicer!!!' "